Stink

(Is something rotten in the State of Denmark?)

Stink

(Is something rotten in the State of Denmark?)

Mac Cambray

Green Dragon Publications

First published in England 2000
by Green Dragon Publications
St Thomas's Square, Monmouth NP5 3ES

Copyright © Mac Cambray

The right of Mac Cambray to be identified as the Author
of this work has been asserted by him in accordance with
the Copyright, Designs and Patents Act 1988.

All rights reserved under international copyright conventions.
No part of this publication may be reproduced, stored
in a retrieval system, copied or transmitted by any means,
electronic, electrostatic, chemical, magnetic tape,
photocopying or otherwise, save with written permission
of the Publishers or in accordance with the provisions
of the Copyright, Designs and Patents Act 1988.

British Library Cataloguing in Publication Data

A catalogue reference for this book is available from the
British Library.

Cambray, Mac
Stink (Is something rotten in the State of Denmark?)

ISBN 0-9539262-0-6

This book is a work of fiction, any similarities to real people or
events is purely accidental.

Set in Monotype Times by
The Studio, Venny Bridge, Exeter.
Printed in Great Britain by
Redwood Books, Trowbridge, Wiltshire.

"This book is dedicated to anyone who thinks they can – and then does".

About the Author

Mac Cambray was born in South Wales in 1942. He was educated at a Cardiff College run by a particularly forceful order of Catholic Brothers. At the age of fifteen he left school with a G.C.E. 'O' level in English Literature and an unnatural inclination for corporal punishment.

Armed with his unexpected academic qualification and an absolute belief in his ability he set out to become a writer of great literary works. Four decades and a skip full of rejection slips later he began to have doubts in the 'O' level examiner's competence.

With the words of his English teacher (nil desperandum) forever branded on his frontal lobes he kept his head down until eventually his standards collapsed into that sewer he calls his imagination. Prior to the publication of this work his greatest achievement was a weekly column in the Bridgend and District Recorder under the heading "Hot Air by Dai".

After one particularly slanderous column Cambray was obliged to leave Bridgend and is now writing action plans for the markets and fairs office of his local authority.

'Stink' is Cambray's first book. If there is any justice in the world it will be his last.

Acknowledgements

Most reputable authors acknowledge the contributions of individuals who have no meaning to the reader whatsoever.

As I was the one, and only one, who slaved for days, weeks, months in front of an intermittently malfunctioning computer screen I am loath to offer salute to anyone else.

However, without the financial courage of Peter Burkhardt of the Green Dragon and Green Dragon Publications, Monmouth, and the eagle-eyed editorial scrutiny of Paul Mahoney of Monmouth Market, this work may have remained in a drawer gathering dust.

Therefore all writs, libel suits and sundry complaints should be aimed entirely at them.

Disclaimer
The characters and collation of events in this book are the products of a disturbed mind and should be discounted as having any relevance to anyone or anything.

1

"Picture the scene Birdman," Dobson said, "there I am, stretched out on Lewington's table, underpants and trousers down around my ankles and shirt up round my neck."

Jack Prosser put down his pint, took a long deep breath and slowly shook his head. Doctor Lewington was not the man you would want hovering over your half naked body about to inspect your full frontals. The younger of the village doctors had gained a reputation for touching and fondling over and above the accepted line of doctoral duties.

In the beginning it was mainly hearsay and conjecture but as the rumour grew so did the queue of women eager to discover whether stripping for a sore throat was par for the course.

It was noted by the regulars in Charlies' bar that there was no accounting for the ways of women or the lengths that they would go to for a quick extra marital thrill. The very same bar room orators failed to notice that it was their own women who were often at the front of the queue.

"Then," continued Dobson, "Lewington picks up my todger and moves it from the downward droop position, so as he could get a better look at my goolies."

Prosser smiled.

"He gets the left one between his thumb and forefinger and starts rolling it around like some captain of industry playing with his executive toy."

Jack's smile changed to a frown. The thought of Ned's left testicle being subjected to such eye watering action sent a shiver down his spine.

"'Any pain?' says Lewington, all sarcastic like."

"What did you say to that?"

"What I said Birdman old pal was – BLOODY HELL – very loudly. Then Lewington says 'Mmm, a bit touchy aren't they Mr. Dobson?'"

"What did you say to that?" Jack repeated.

"I said, 'Your nuts would be touchy if they had been toe-poked by a cretinous old hag'."

'Who was drunk at the time,' offered Jack.

"Who was absolutely rat arsed at the time," Dobson said, frowning at the painful memory of it.

The conversation came to a halt. Dobson suspended the account of his visit to the doctors and drifted into his own mini daydream. For the next few moments the pair seemed content to pass the time supping their beers and mulling over the bizarre events of the weekend, Jack taking alternate pulls on his well lit briar pipe.

* * *

To most people living in the village of Monks End, 'rat arsed cretinous old hag' was Ned's expected description of Gwendolyn Fors-Bowers.

This degrading and malicious title, however, should not be taken as wholly correct with regard to the lady in question. Spending most of her waking hours in a perpetual mood of relaxed conviviality, partly due, it must be said in her defence, to the lengthy preparation of Ned's evening meal in a kitchen brimming with assorted wines and cooking sherries, is not sufficient reason for Dobson to elevate her to the state of rat arsedness. That phrase, therefore, must be accepted as a cruel overstatement on Ned's part.

Gwendolyn had been educated at Cheltenham Ladies, was fluent in French and German, a cordon bleu cook, an expert seamstress and as the daughter of wealthy Wiltshire landowner, Randolph Fors-Bowers, came from a background a good many stops up the line from her detractor's own station in life. If it is true that into every life a little rain must fall then into Gwendolyn Fors-Bowers' privileged life came a downpour and permanent trough of low pressure in the shape of Ned Dobson. Known throughout the county by his inane weekly article in the Gloucestershire Record under the banner heading of Dobsons' Revenge.

To blandly state that Ned had fallen into Gwendolyn's life is, as the more intelligent amongst you would realise, not the whole story. The full and unabridged account may one day emerge for all to digest. Until then the bones of the gossip at the time are these:

Twenty five years ago Ned, then aged 33, was on weekend manoeuvres with the Territorial Army on Salisbury Plain. He had joined the T.A. soon after giving up playing rugby. His rugby playing days, as the Monks Enders' short and stocky scrum half, ended when, trapped under a mound of sweating heaving forwards he got the impression, not to mention feeling, that someone was trying to bite his dick off. Enough was enough, thought Ned. His todger had a very full diary and it could not afford to be out of service for medical treatment. The volunteer Army offered him about the same amount of drinking and lecherous camaraderie, but without any great risk to limbs or vital organs. It was a reasonable trade off.

Twenty five years ago, during an evening of rest and recuperation trawling the local pubs, he met and fell for Gwendolyn's sixteen-year-old rebellious daughter Magenta. This single act alone Gwendolyn could have dealt with in the age-old upper crust manner. In fact, money was on the point of changing hands until the unruly Magenta complicated the situation by announcing that not only did she fancy this uncouth, twice her age, lower class upstart, but was up the bung and due to calf in three months time. At which Gwendolyn flung her arms in the air and in keeping with her rude daughter's mode of expression proclaimed her feelings on the subject with that distinctly unladylike phrase – "Oh Bollocks!".

It was to be one of life's bittersweet moments for Ned. True, he was about to gain the hand of the girl of his lustful dreams but in doing so he had to turn his back on the dab in the fist on offer from her mother. A woman just a few years older than him and about to become his Mother-in-Law.

There was no sign of Magenta's father. Indeed, any mention of this missing link was guaranteed to bring the most sparkling of conversations to an abrupt end.

Unknown to Dobson it was not only Magenta who had gone glassy eyed at the sight of a uniform. Gwendolyn had had a similar instant reaction sixteen years earlier.

It is a biological fact as any gynaecologist worth his salt will tell you, that an average couple intent on producing offspring may take up to four or five months of intensive humping before the required result is achieved. In both mother and daughter Fors-Bowers' case a closer estimate would be four or five knee trembling minutes. The leafy lane that ran along the eastern edge of Randolph Fors-Bowers' land had been witness to both copulations. As both the men involved were in uniform, their deeds were accomplished with military like precision. Hands up – two three. Down – two three. In – two three. Out – two three. Thanks – two three. And, in the case of Magenta's bunk doing father, GOODBYE – two three.

In fairness to Gwendolyn Fors-Bowers she would never have entertained the thought of fraternising with a Uniform so low down the scale as a weekend T.A. volunteer. Dropping them for anyone less than an officer was simply not the done thing. The well bred, after all, must maintain certain standards. It was not many days after Magenta's exciting news of her impending motherhood that Gwendolyn took to drinking. Her figure ballooned and dark circles appeared under her pale blue eyes – quite a pleasant match in fact. It came as no surprise to anyone when Randolph Fors-Bowers, renowned for being totally temperate and deeply entrenched chapel, banished Gwendolyn and pregnant grand-daughter Magenta with – 'Never darken my doorstep again'. A speech that may have lacked imagination and creativity, but was none the less effective.

Dobson, with an eye for the future had no hesitation in taking Magenta and her mother under his working class wing. He held great store in the indisputable physical fact that blood was thicker than water. He clung like a limpet to the hope that the wealthy Randolph would one day relent, returning the ladies to the status quo and him to a status dreamed of.

How wrong he was dear reader. It is now twenty-five hope sapping years later. Magenta's impregnation had proved to be a mischief-making falsehood on her part. Randolph, the old bugger, is in his eighty-ninth year and showing no signs of forgiveness. Ned's one-time rock solid beliefs and hopes are beginning to creak and groan.

The early libidinous rewards for taking a wife seventeen years his junior have long been cancelled out by the penalty of her mother being just three years his senior. Living with a Mother-in-Law who completely outclassed him and a wife whose rebellious nature showed no signs of abating and had discovered that her sex appeal had value – approximately 20 pounds a shag – has frayed his marriage bonds to within a whisker of snapping. He has survived these torrid and tormented years by dreaming of the two thousand acres of Wiltshire field and woodland that would one day, possibly, maybe, fingers crossed, fall into his lap.

That dream is fading. Has he wasted the best years of his life on a lost cause? It does not bear thinking about. But think about it he does, continually. Here he is, in the twilight of his career, a social, political and environmental commentator on some grotty little freebee. Was this all that life was going to offer him? The more he thought the more testy he became. It showed in his vitriolic articles in the Record, in his acrimonious conversations with the mob in the bar of the Feathers, and visitors to the Dobson family home could sense it in the tense, almost apocalyptic atmosphere that prevailed within. Life there had arrived at a very fragile Modus Vivendi indeed.

Years of stress and aggravation had turned Ned Dobson into a beer swilling randy old bigot – characteristics not entirely unknown amongst the more senior members of the journalistic profession. He had arrived at a time in his life when he was no longer prepared to sit back and allow his fate to roll along unchecked. If it needed a nudge or two in order for it to produce the goods then a nudge or two it would get. He decided that any outward signs of family unity would score him points with Randolph the disciplinarian. Ned had led a very singular life. He had gained a reputation as a heavy drinker and frequent fornicator. Perhaps gained is an inappropriate word. Earned may be the one needed here for Ned worked hard at his reputation. Not so much at his drinking, that came easily. Fornicating needed a little more effort. He had moved on from being short and stocky to short and plump-ish. His eyes now required the assistance of a pair of spectacles and what was once a black moustache had turned completely grey. Pulling the birds needed a little more guile these days. Ned had an abundance of guile and used it – abundantly. Magenta and her mother, they too had led singular lives, though it must be said Gwendolyn had almost given up any possibility of a sexual encounter as a lost cause. Until she crossed paths with Alan Johnson, the local Member of Parliament. Alan was a gentleman, well read and well bred. The moment she set eyes on him her torch was lit.

Magenta on the other hand had turned sex into an art form. She patrolled her favoured Gloucester public houses, as she had done for over twenty years, in fishnet stockings, red leather mini skirt and black lycra top, offering her form of art to whoever would bid. By day she was Magenta Dobson, part time sales assistant at Monks End's grocery shop. Three evenings a week she was Tania offering a more intimate service to her customers.

If it meant him (Ned) and them (Gwendolyn and Magenta) turning over new leafs in order to get his (Ned's) hands on Randolph's wealth then that is what they would to do, or, at least appear to do.

Family unity would be the beginning. He would go to great pains to prove to Randolph that the three of them were one happy family. Unfortunately, his effort that weekend had caused him greater pain than he had anticipated.

It had been an exceptional summer. July looked like being one of the hottest on record. That Friday evening Ned, as usual, had gone straight from work for a couple of cooling beers at Charlie Harries' pub, the Feathers. As usual, he was joined by his mate Birdman Jack Prosser. Jack was not only the local amateur ornithologist as his nickname implied but also the Record's photographer. As usual, the pair drank two pints of Charlie's best bitter before leaving for their neighbouring homes and their evening meals. At five minutes to seven Ned was turning the key in his front door. By seven o'clock he was sitting down to the most sumptuous presentation of food that any man could ask for after a days work.

A table set to perfection. Mendelssohn's violin concerto in E minor gently relaxing the mood, Gwendolyn had been relaxed for quite a while. Ned, Magenta and Gwendolyn dined on: Chilled Lemon Soup. Veal Escalopes with Vermouth and Orange. Fresh Fruit Pavlova. An assorted cheese board followed by cups of freshly ground coffee and mint chocolates completed the meal. As usual, Gwendolyn served the meal. As usual, there was little in the way of conversation and compliments would not, usually, be offered. But for something to be usual there has to be an unusual.

That evening:

"That was a wonderful meal Mother-in-Law." Ned always addressed Gwendolyn with her full and respectful title when speaking to her face to face. If she ever discovered what he called her at the pub he would receive a look capable of turning granite into dust.

"I was thinking."

Gwendolyn and Magenta eyed him with suspicion. He never exposed his thoughts to them, ever.

"There's a function this evening down at Charlie – er Mr. Harries' place The Three Feathers. He's having the name of the place changed. There will be councillors and business people coming. Denzil has asked me to cover it for the paper. I was wondering if you would both like to join me?"

Gwendolyn stared at him with a look that was on the edge of astonishment.

"You want ME to go to a public house?"

Magenta frowned.

"Most of the Chamber of Trade are going." Ned continued.

Magenta brightened. Some of the younger shop managers were quite horny.

"And Alan Johnston, the Member of Parliament, he will be there"

Now Gwendolyn brightened. She had met Alan at an old school friend's garden party the previous summer. She was getting on well with him until she had slipped into the garden pond. Her friends and their hoity husbands watched with amusement as Alan helped her clamber out covered in weed and spitting goldfish. As she flopped gasping on the lawn like a beached whale, her soaked cotton dress revealing every crevice and mound of her bottom and breasts, her friends and their hoity husbands knew that any chance of Gwendolyn pulling the local member had just sunk with all hands. Ned had heard the story and hoped that she would see this night as an opportunity to regain some lost ground with the man. The bait had been set.

"Jack Prosser is coming to take some photographs," Ned offered, hopeful that a picture of Gwendolyn with a Member of Parliament would help his cause with Randolph. "I could make sure he takes one of you and Alan together. Alan's tipped for a post in the Cabinet you know. Tell you what. I'll clear the table and wash the dishes while you two go and put your best frocks on. How does that sound?"

It sounded incredible, but the fish was hooked and Gwendolyn was the first to move.

* * *

Charlie Harries, landlord and owner of Monks End's one and only pub was not a Gloucestershire man. He ran one of the best pubs for miles around so he was accepted as one of the lads of course, but he was not a natural born local. Charlie came from – well, truth to tell none of the regulars actually knew where Charlie Harries came from. It was rumoured that he was a Surreyish sort of bloke, no one was quite sure. The landlord was also a confirmed bachelor. To the regulars that elegant and old fashioned phrase meant that Charlie never had to put up with the encumbrances and ceaseless demands of a wife and kids. Charles Harries had inherited a substantial sum on the death of a relative. Part of it bought and paid for The Feathers at Monks End. The remainder, and quite a chunky remainder it was, he invested in stocks, bonds and shares.

The Three Feathers had been The Three Feathers for as long as anyone could remember. There was a degree of adverse muttering among the regulars when word got out that Charlie intended to change its name. But it was his pub, he had made his mind up and planning had been granted.

The old plume of feathers sign had been removed. Its' place to be taken by a scene illustrating a gentleman of mature years in mid eighteenth century dress, sat in front of a blazing log fire. A pewter mug full of frothing ale in one hand and a long stemmed clay pipe in the other. There were claims by the few who had seen it, prior to the evening's unveiling ceremony, that the features of the man on the sign were not unlike Ned's.

Charlie stoutly denied this. Pointing out that Ned was a non-smoker. However, since Ned had began mentioning his pub in his weekly column the landlord had become an avid reader and great fan of the writer. The new name of his pub was to be 'Ye Olde Tippling Philosopher'.

It did not occur to Charlie that his regulars would shorten this grand title of his beloved establishment to the 'Tip'. He kept one of the best pints of bitter in the county so no malice would have been intended. Nevertheless, whenever he heard his pub being called by the shortened version of its full name it never failed to hurt. Charlie was a large and jovial man. A kind and gentle man. A much appreciated man. His pub was one of the last remaining establishments of its kind untouched by themes and fads. It had one bar and a function room. The latter being available free of charge for parties and wedding receptions, provided those who wanted it did their own catering.

Like most of the buildings in the village square the Tippling Philosopher was built of Cotswold stone that had been hewn from local quarries more than two hundred years earlier. The bar room was oblong in shape. On the left-hand side of the room was a large fireplace around which were a cluster of tables and chairs. The table in the far corner was where Ned, Jack Prosser, Sparkie Lee and Jake Brown sat, drank, and set the world to rights. In front of the windows and along the right-hand wall were an assortment of benches tables chairs and stools available for the less important members of the Tip's congregation. From his own position behind the bar Charlie could look out across the square. Its centrepiece was a First World War memorial cross with a base of three stone steps. The steps were originally designed to receive wreaths and flowers but were now used more frequently as the seats of a meeting place by Monks End's younger generation. Apart from the Tippling Philosopher the only other businesses in the square were; Sparkie's electrical repair shop, a post office that sold sweets and greetings cards, a grocers that doubled as the wine lodge and the Rajputana King Balti Take Away. The remaining buildings consisted of terraced houses and the Ebenezer Chapel which nestled up against the Tip's gable end. Between Sparkie's shop and the post office was a lane which led to a large Victorian house. Here lived Doctor Phillips who, with his younger partner Doctor Lewington, held a daily surgery there. South of the square was an estate of pre-war council houses. To the west a small development of private houses. Here lived Vaughan and Adele Ames in a detached four bedroom mock Tudor house. Vaughan Ames owned The Gloucestershire Clarion. Come out of 'Ye Olde Tippling Philosopher' and turn left past the Ebenezer, left again and up the hill, and you will, if you looked closely through the cluster of horse chestnut and sycamore trees, spot Denzil Wynstanly's tiny two bedroom home. Denzil owned The Gloucestershire Record. Wynstanly and Ames were desperately trying to put each other out of business. At the top of the hill are a row of six cottages, known locally as – The Cottages. Ned, Magenta and Gwendolyn lived at No. 4. Jack and Agnes Prosser at No. 5.

The distance, from No. 4 The Cottages, Monks End, to Charlie Harries' pub was less than three-quarters of a mile. Ned always walked it.

That evening, Gwendolyn insisted on calling a taxi from Gloucester. A taxi that was timed to deliver them to the establishment just a few moments behind schedule. Gwendolyn knew that those who arrived too early would have no one there to greet them. Those who arrived a little late would be seen arriving. Such is the value of a public school education.

As the taxi pulled up Charlie Harries rushed forward.

"Ned my friend, and Magenta AND Mrs. Fors-Bowers. This is a pleasure. Welcome, welcome. Come and meet our Member of Parliament. He has kindly agreed to unveil our new sign."

"Mr. Johnston and I have already made our acquaintances." Gwendolyn announced grandly.

Alan Johnston smiled. "Good evening Mrs. Fors-Bowers. I am so glad to see that you have recovered from that unfortunate accident. Garden ponds can be quite dangerous. We should all be very wary of them on such convivial occasions."

The gathering moved to the front door of the building, above which the new sign hung. It was covered in a red velvet drape. A plaited gold tassel, when pulled, would unveil the sign for all to marvel at. Gwendolyn positioned herself towards the back of the crowd. In front of her were the right Worshipful Mayor of Gloucester, the Mayor of Cheltenham and a group of City Councillors. All were eager to be prominently pictured by the posse of photographers jostling in front of them. Gwendolyn's strategy had never failed her yet. It did not fail her on this occasion. Ever the gentleman it was Charlie Harries who noticed.

"Mrs. Fors-Bowers! Please come to the front. Let the lady through gentlemen, let her through. Here! Mrs. Fors-Bowers, please stand next to Mr. Johnston."

Alan Johnston smiled. Gwendolyn smiled. Jack Prosser, and the rest, flashed away while Johnston held his hand on the tassel. A quick pull revealed all, to nods of approval. Gwendolyn's smile sagged when she saw the face of the character on the pub's new sign.

"It's HIM," she thought. "If that's not him, I will eat my mink"

Charlie Harries prided himself on running an old fashioned public house. There were no bar snacks or micro-waved traditional Sunday lunches at £5.95 a head. The best that his patrons could expect would be crisps, peanuts and possibly a slice of Gala pork pie on Saturday nights. As for entertainment they had to make their own. Something which Ned and the rest had become masters at over the years.

However, to mark this extra special occasion the landlord had engaged a company of high class caterers to provide an expensive buffet. Also, and believing that it was the right thing to do, he had installed some kareoke equipment to help jolly up the evening.

Not wanting to have forked out a such substantial amount in vain Charlie spent most of the evening filling up plates and encouraging everyone to show off their wonderful rustic voices. Many did, including Ned who had always fancied himself as a singer. He would never be the next Sinatra but he made a reasonable fist of one of the great man's songs. He sang 'Come fly with me come fly let's fly away –'. There were few regulars who did not notice the eye contact he was making with Rosie the barmaid.

Gwendolyn also had a fine voice. A near perfect soprano which she kept it in trim singing along to her Gilbert and Sullivan recordings whilst preparing Fricandeau of Veal, or some other eupeptic crushing culinary extravaganza. When the need arose Gwendolyn was nothing if not a trouper. Having committed herself to slumming it with Dobson she felt duty bound to give the evening her full attention. She needed little encouragement from the floor. Alan would be watching. Besides, the recipe for the Veal escalopes with vermouth and Orange had called for a quarter of a pint of the wine, which is exactly what it got. The remainder of the bottle was whizzing around her circulatory system. Four large gin and tonics had already joined forces with it and another was on it's way, so there was no stopping her.

Her performance of 'Rocking All Over The World' was spectacular. It had her audience up on their feet clapping and shouting for more. Could she match it? She did, with a spontaneous and unaccompanied version of the 'Can Can'. Her kicks got higher and higher, exposing more and more yardage of knee length knickers, much to the ribald amusement of the regulars and the unusual embarrassment of Magenta.

Ned was given instructions to bring the show to a close and was helped on his way with a shove in the back. His stumbling arrival centre stage coincided with one of Gwendolyn's high kicks, which he stopped in the crutch. This fierce collision of upwardly mobile shoe with his scrotum sack not only caused him considerable pain but also dislodged most of the wax from his ears. It was widely agreed that the stream of vituperative that followed was some of the most colourful ever heard in the bar.

Alan Johnston, Member of Parliament, just smiled.

The incident left Ned nursing a pair of bruised bollocks. He had received no mercy or words of comfort from any of his mates at the Tip and could expect little better from the staff of the Record when he turned up for work on Monday morning.

2

Denzil Wynstanly sat at his large oak and maple desk drumming his fat fingers on its smooth surface. The tiny beads of perspiration on his forehead were quickly turning into large droplets of sweat. Soon their increasing volume would allow them to break free and roll down his fat cheeks to drip onto the stain on his desk. The desk was new, Denzil Wynstanly sweated a lot.

'Damn Ames. Damn his smarmy hide. He'll pay for this. I'll wipe him out – if it takes every penny – I'll finish him – I'll finish him.'

Denzil's desk was plumb in the middle of the polished mahogany floor ensuring that he was the very epicentre of this spacious and profuse office. On the oak panelled walls around him hung an assortment of framed photographs. Each one a picture of himself in various civic and casual poses. Wynstanly was a big man. He carried his weight well for someone who stood six feet tall, weighed seventeen and a half stone and had just past his fifty-fourth birthday. He was also a very good dancer, light on his feet as many larger men are. The bulk above his knees was counterbalanced by calves of sprung steel which allowed his feet to twinkle and his body to sway as he sashayed his partner around the dance floor. His dancing partner would not be Mrs. Wynstanly. There was no Mrs. Wynstanly. His partner would be any of the wives attending the function that Denzil had turned up at, to show off his ballroom skills. Being able to dance was Denzil's only contribution to social intercourse. The wives enjoyed dancing with him in spite of his excessive perspiration. Throughout the dance they would covertly wipe the sweat, transferred from his hand to theirs, onto their evening gowns and dresses. After a particularly vigorous sashay drops of Denzil's sweat would splatter onto their cheeks and eyebrows. Nevertheless, as their own husbands could only clump about the dance floor like rhythmically dyslexic puppets the wives were prepared to put up with the occasional salty shower. But when the dancing ended, when the last chords of the last waltz floated away Denzil's style and charisma floated away with them. He returned to being tedious. As boring as a sun dried dog turd, brittle and with no affable substance whatsoever. No one spoke to him unless they needed to talk business. A Chamber of Trade member or a fellow Rotarian, anyone. Anyone who would rather give him an order for a half page advertisement at a function than attend Denzil's office and risk being verbally bludgeoned into taking a full page. He did a lot of business at these events. The deals were done quickly. A fact that he put down to his superior selling technique.

Denzil had never married. He had never felt the need to. His work was his life. As the only son of Bill and Evelyn Wynstanly he had inherited the family hardware business in Downend, Bristol. He sold the three bedroom family home that he had lived in all his life and moved into a room above the shop that his father had used to store junk in. Denzil had his father's skill as a handyman, and his size. Bill Wynstanly had also been a large man and sweated a lot when he was working. By day Denzil worked and sweated in the hardware shop. By night he worked and sweated converting the two stories above the shop into flats. When he had finished he rented one flat out and lived by himself in the other. With the capital from the sale of the family home, the rent from the flat, the profit from the shop and no dependants Denzil was financially secure. Most men would have settled for that. Denzil Wynstanly was not cut out to settle for anything. He bought another hardware shop. By day he managed his shop and made regular sweaty telephone calls to the manager of the second shop urging him to work hard and increase the profits. By night Denzil worked and sweated at the second business converting the rooms above the shop into flats which he rented out. With the capital from the sale of the family home, rent from three flats, profits from two hardware shops and no dependants Denzil was now even more financially secure. Most men would have settled for that. Denzil was not cut out to settle for anything. He bought a third hardware shop. By day he managed his shop and made double the number of sweaty telephone calls to the managers of the other shops urging them to work hard and increase the profits. By night he worked at the third premises converting the rooms above the shop into flats which he rented out. With the capital from the sale of the – Oh! you know the rest.

But Denzil was not happy with what he had. He became disenchanted with selling nuts and bolts, bags of nails, gallons of paraffin and cutting keys for old ladies. He wanted a posher sort of empire. He sold his flats and hardware businesses, lock stock and key cutting machine. With the capital from the sale of the family home, the flats and his brown overalled empire he bought the ailing advertising free-sheet The Gloucestershire Record, and a two bedroom cottage in the Cotswold village of Monks End.

Under Denzil's command the paper's weekly circulation rose from eight thousand copies to sixty thousand copies, with an advertising revenue that larger organisations could only dream of. Work was his life and success his very life blood. He craved success. He demanded success. He intended to buy up every advertising paper in the South and West of England including, and especially, Vaughan Ames' Clarion. He applied to join the newly opened local golf club. It would increase his contacts and he would become even more successful.

The very day he received notification that he had been accepted as a member, he also noticed flecks of grey beginning to appear in his hair. No signs of baldness, but definite signs of greying. Vaughan Ames was grey.

Denzil decided that he would not be – ever.

There are times in every man's life, even single men, when a woman's guidance can be essential. If there had been a woman by his side when he chose his hair dye, she would have guided his hand away from the bright concoction that he eventually bought. To him, the colour on the box looked identical to that of his own hair. When he took the dye home and applied it, the end result looked more like sombre orange. Wynstanly failed to notice the end result. His only concern was that he could no longer see flecks of grey. Sombre orange would, from then on, be his colour.

Whether it was his newly coloured hair, or, that he lived alone, or, that his private life was a mystery, or, maybe, a combination of all three, the question of Denzil Wynstanly's sexuality suddenly became an interesting topic of conversation. A question totally without credence and born entirely out of malicious curiosity. The photographs on the wall of his office played their part in reminding visitors that they were in the company of a pillar of the community. Here, shaking hands with local M.P. Alan Johnson at a civic luncheon. Here, applauding the Mayor of Cheltenham's opening drive at a charity golf tournament and here, starting the Record's Annual Fun Run. An event which he alone had devised and insisted that the entire compliment of Record staff take part in. Including his journalist Ned Dobson, whose requests for being excused on the grounds of having bunions and irregular bowels where always ignored.

The Record fun run raised many thousands of charitable pounds. There was much glory and kudos to be gained by the sponsor and organiser – otherwise Denzil would not have sponsored and organised it. It was glory and kudos that he gained with the merest amount of perspiration in comparison to the volumes that exuded from the pores of those who did the running and, therefore, the actual raising of cash. Besides, Denzil could sweat well enough without having to put himself through a 6 km fun run at the height of summer. And he had noticed that there were many brave Gloucestershire souls at the end of the course and in various states of collapse who had realised, all too painfully, that fun running was in fact not much fun at all.

Each year the Record's photographer was on hand to photograph Wynstanly. Once at the start and again at the finish where he, Denzil Wynstanly, sponsor of the race and owner of the Gloucestershire Record, proudly presented the prizes. As the winner invariably turned out to be a junior reporter on the rival Clarion it was the start picture that got the nod for publication.

Denzil eased his corpulent frame back into the studded tan leather arm chair, his most favourite piece of office furniture. He had rejected out of hand Messrs. Kimble and Dougherty's suggestion of a designer swivel chair on the grounds that as owner of the Record he was a newspaper magnate not "a bloody commodities broker".

The question in Denzil Wynstanly's mind, this fine July Monday morning, had nothing to do with chairs, swivel or otherwise, but everything to do with how to regain the initiative in his war with the Clarion. How to put one over on Vaughan Ames? The answer to the first part being finely balanced with the answer to the second as Ames was the owner of the opposing paper.

This was not a war of circulation, as is customary between sparring newspapers. Circulation was not a problem for either paper. They were both free-sheets and got stuffed into people's letter boxes whether they wanted them or not.

This conflict was far more important. This was a war of prestige, of high profiles and of standing in the community. With the winner being feted, back slapped and hand shook at functions and gatherings throughout the area. It was galling for Wynstanly to have to sit and watch Ames lapping up the adulation. Galling, yes, but not nearly as distressing as losing advertising revenue.

Advertising revenue was money, and money meant success – to Denzil Wynstanly.

The Clarion was winning the war hands down. Not because its advertising rates were cheaper, but because Vaughan Ames had stumbled on to a formula that set his paper above the rest. Editorial content in weekly free-sheets does not make for riveting and mind stretching reading. It is a rarely spoken fact that the only people who read weekly advertising papers are the advertisers themselves and then only to read their own advertisement. When Ames discovered that he had more space between the advertisements than usual he employed an out of work journalist, Maxwell Lomax, to write a column for him. Lomax's first column, Maxwell's Moments, was loaded with pith and wit and drew heavily on his experiences as a national journalist. Lomax had a great store of stories about goth and fetishly inclined Cabinet Ministers, revolting back bench politicians and riotous showbiz parties. The story of the goth and fetishly inclined Cabinet Minister who came face to face with one of his own revolting back benchers at a riotous showbiz party would have to be handled carefully if he ever got the chance to publish it. Nevertheless the first of Maxwell's Moments, although discreet, was a success.

To his regular readers it appeared that Ames had done them a great service by upgrading the usual editorial dross that they had to plough through. The clarion's post bag was filled with praise and acclamation for Vaughan Ames's initiative in employing Lomax. The best of the letters featured prominently on the Clarion's Letters page. Lomax's articles were syndicated, at a fee, to hundreds of free-sheets around the country. At the bottom of each publication Ames insisted on the tag THIS ARTICLE FIRST APPEARED IN THE GLOUCESTERSHIRE CLARION.

Ames, The Clarion and Lomax were riding on a crest of a wave and advertisers in and around Gloucester and Cheltenham were not slow to realise where they should place their adverts in order to get the best return. Few, if any, knew or cared that Ames had stumbled into the spotlight entirely by accident.

As he sat at his desk Denzil continued his thoughtful search for an answer. An antidote to Ames' sudden surge of popularity and his own paper's sudden drop in takings. He believed that he had misjudged his readers. He had done them an injustice by allowing his own journalist, Ned Dobson, to pay too much attention to the local sports teams, the number of out of town shopping malls, the quality of the beer at the local pub in Monks End – on which Dobson could write a thesis of honours degree standard. He had demanded that Dobson produce an article of his own. It would be headlined Dobson's Revenge. It would be political, sharp and incisive. The chances of Dobson writing anything politically sharp and incisive or indeed writing anything worth reading at all were slimmer than an anorexic fag paper.

In his first piece he opted for a hatchet job on the character of local Independent councillor Ms. Terri Wilkinson. Ms. Wilkinson was a vegetarian. An extreme vegetarian. She could smell a product containing even the smallest amount of animal fat from fifty metres. At town twinnings, civic functions and the County Hall cafeteria she insisted on enforcing her culinary attitude. She wore long coats, tracker boots and her hair short and spikey. In the first of Dobson's Revenges Ned labelled her; Councillor Terri the mad lesbian veggy (Allegedly).

Ms. Wilkinson was the daughter of one of the biggest used car dealers in Gloucestershire. Wynstanly lost another advertiser, but gained the threat of a law suit. Life can be delightfully even handed when it wants to.

Dobson's efforts continued to be more chaff than wheat. Whilst rummaging through the draw of his desk that held his collection of soft porn magazines he unearthed copies of The Citizen's charter. Great, he thought. I'll give this a shagging.

21

"Good morning Mrs. Rogers. Your usual?"

"Oh yes please Mr. Clark, 2 lb of scrag end and six pork and beef thank you."

"A wonderful thing this Citizens Charter Mrs. Rogers".

"Truly wonderful Mr. Clark. Do you know, if I were to step outside your shop and be knocked down there would be an ambulance along in fourteen minutes?"

"Truly wonderful Mrs. Rogers. That will be £1.95 thank you."

"Can you put it on the slate please Mr. Clark?"

"I'd rather not Mrs. Rogers, not if you are going to get knocked down the minute you leave my shop thank you."

"Was it not amazing?" Dobson pronounced, "that compensation could be claimed for trains that were late, that motorways would soon be free from cones, that gas fitters would turn up within a month of them saying they would and, most comforting of all, that hospitals would do their level best to see before you pegged it. Read it in the Citizen's Charter. Wonderful thing that Charter – WONDERFUL".

Whether the Citizen's Charter was being given a first or even second thought by the countries citizens is not worth giving a first or second thought to. The bald fact remained that Dobson's work could not hold a candle to that of Lomax's. Wynstanly was looking more and more like the pilot of a lead balloon.

It was becoming too much for Denzil. The repercussions were beginning to take effect. In the members bar at the golf club he had to elbow his way into pockets of conversation even more vigorously than usual. Vaughan Ames, on the other hand, always had a clutch of members around him, hanging on his every word.

Like Denzil, Ames was a tall man. Unlike Denzil he was slim, athletic looking, constantly tanned and with a full head of brushed back silver grey hair. He dressed immaculately and expensively. By day in hand made suits purchased from a bespoke tailor situated above an antique dealer in London's Old Brompton Road. During the evening, smartly casual. Always with a shirt and tie, never in slacks and sweater. An assortment of gold cuff links and an ever present gold watch were further hints that this man had money. He was also experienced in the world of advertising. He owned a design company that created artwork for advertisers. He had a modest but profitable portfolio of clients, some of them national. Buying The Clarion, a weekly advertising paper, was an obvious additional string. A lot of his design company's artwork appeared in the Clarion and some even in the Record, but Wynstanly was not smart enough to realise that the invoices were coming from one of his arch rival's own companies. Wynstanly's arrival had irritated Ames immensely. Not because The Record had, at first, taken some of his advertisers from him, there was more than enough business for both papers. Ames's irritation was of a more personal nature. How dare such a fat ignorant slob of a man cross business swords with him. How dare Wynstanly try and join with the county's elite social circle and let his fat sweaty hands touch the hands of the women who Ames himself had handled, fondled even.

Vaughan Ames was a charmer, he oozed confidence. He was always smiling and although he was married he frequently hunted and caught any attractive woman that took his fancy. For Vaughan Ames every day was ladies day. Adele Ames was also one of the county's beautiful people. An elegant woman. A career woman. As a buyer for a national fashion house her work frequently took her to London, Paris and Rome. She ignored her husband's philandering, partly because her work kept her away from home a lot and partly because she had at least two lovers of her own around Europe. The Ames' had no children.

Keeping in with the golf club in crowd was not the most pressing of Denzil's worries. The Clarion's current wave of popularity and the disastrous drop in the Record's advertising revenue had highlighted a more pressing matter. On his desk was a reminder from his bank manager. For the second time that month the bank felt obliged to draw Denzil's attention to the fact that his company's overdraft had passed its limit. The bank was looking forward to a significant reduction – soon.

If the paper's downward spiral continued then he would have to make some hard decisions. A cut in salaries? – the staffs of course, not his. Redundancies? – that wouldn't do his already waning popularity any good at all. But if the Record's difficult financial situation were to be improved what else could he do?

The letter from the bank and the continuing depletion of advertising revenue had forced Denzil into a moment of powerful concentration. Then as though he was travelling down his very own road to Damascus, he was suddenly struck by, what he believed was, a blinding flash of inspirational light.

"That's it!" He slammed his fat fist down onto his desk, causing his morning cup of coffee to leap into the air and spill over a pile of advertising copy. "If it's politics the fools want then they shall have it. And, they shall read it in MY paper." He grabbed the internal telephone.

"Sophie – get Dobson up here straight away and bring a cloth with you, someone has spilt coffee over my desk – be sharp girl, be sharp."

Denzil's fat fingers began drumming up a storm. The damp patch on his desk was spreading. He now sat at there with a very different feeling in his bones as he waited for the arrival of his senior journalist.

3

Sophie Davies was twenty two years of age, tall, slender and Wynstanly's very efficient right hand. She passed Ned on the stairs as he was making slow and painful progress in his ascent to Denzil's office.

"He's in a mood again this morning Mr. Dobson. I heard about your accident on the weekend. That must have been painful. Getting better are they?" She asked with a smile.

"Some gentle massaging might speed up the recovery rate." Ned said, hopefully.

"Cheeky! I can't stop, he's spilt his coffee again. I'll talk to you later."

"Cheers."

Ned stopped to study her long shapely legs. They appeared to be making determined efforts to escape from her short tight skirt as she took the steps two at a time. He would have jumped at the chance of helping them out but a sharp jabbing pain in his genitals reminded him that his Mother-in-Law's right foot had put paid to any sort of jumping for a week or so.

Sophie, cloth in hand, entered Wynstanly's office and began to mop up the pool of coffee.

"Shall I get this copy reset?"

"No! Use it as it is. Where the devil is Dobson?" Denzil's fingers had ceased their impatient tattoo on his desk. Their performance had been replaced by some impatient knuckle rapping.

"I passed him on the stairs. He's having a bit of trouble getting around – an accident on the weekend."

"I suppose that dim-wit of a wife of his ran over his foot again did she?" Denzil said, referring to an incident involving Magenta's lack of driving expertise.

"No, not his foot. I think the problem is a bit higher

up his leg this time – here he is now. Shall I bring two fresh cups?"

"What for?"

"Just the one then."

Ned was about to sink into the chair in front of Wynstanly's desk, following his painful ascent, when some inner instinct told him that he would not be staying. He remained standing.

"Dobson –." Denzil stopped in mid-sentence. He had become aware that his employee was standing in front of him, slightly stooped and with his legs apart. His right hand was apparently cradling his parts.

"Why are you holding your crotch?" Wynstanly's eyes narrowed. "You haven't picked up some sexually transmitted disease have you? It wouldn't surprise me if you had the way you carry on. I don't know how you get away with it at your age."

Ned's libido did not know what time of day it was never mind that it was fast approaching its fifty-ninth birthday. He was, as many of his contemporaries wished they still were, as randy as an eighteen-year-old. He was, like Vaughan Ames, an outrageous womaniser. But whereas Ames restricted his conquests to attractive and intelligent females, Ned went after anything in a skirt.

"Oh no! No sir." Ned said, quickly removing his hand form his aching testes. "It was an accident, at the weekend."

"Don't tell me she ran over your balls this time. She ought to, you deserve it.'

"No. It wasn't the wife this time."

Not the wife this time –? Denzil was tempted to pursue the story to its undoubtedly interesting conclusion but there were far more important matters to get underway.

He fixed an inquiring eye on to his paper's social, political and environmental commentator before firing his question.

"How much do you know about the Maastricht Treaty?"

Ned stared at him. The Maastricht Treaty? The Treaty of Maastricht? The Maas –. He tried to reassemble his scattering brain cells. Has Denzil gone off his head? Has all the agro with Ames and the Clarion finally caused him to flip his lid? What does he mean, what do I know about the Maastricht Treaty? What does ANYBODY know about the Maastricht Treaty?

On 7th of February 1992 the Heads of State of twelve European Community countries were photographed, smiling and confident, in Maastricht, the capital of Limburg province SE Netherlands. On behalf of their Governments they had drawn up a treaty. It was to become known as The Treaty of Maastricht. A treaty that was intended to shape the future of the European Continent and all its people.

Immediately Denmark, France and Ireland held referendums on the Treaty. Their populations were briefed on the nature of the document and its intentions. The French and the Irish gave it a thumbs up, voting in its favour. The Danes threatened to upset the European apple cart by voting "NO" on Maastricht. Later, at the second time of asking, a narrow "YES" was recorded.

In Britain the majority of people, including Ned Dobson, had only the vaguest idea of the meaning of "Maastricht".

"Well sir – it's a er –". Ned stumbled. "That is to say it's a treaty that er –"

"Just as I thought," Denzil proclaimed triumphantly. "You know absolutely bugger all about it just like the rest of the country". He pointed a fat sweaty finger at his journalist. "The Maastricht Treaty is probably the most important document since – since Magna Carta. I intend to run a series of articles outlining all the salient points, in full. This is a multicultural country so we shall run them in English and er! – all the rest." Denzil waved his fat right arm airily. "It is just what our readers want, no, it's what the whole of the country wants. There is not enough political nous around. We are going to

27

rectify that, understand? There are millions of people out there who need to be politically educated. Ames' writer is just scratching the tip of the iceberg. This country is begging for more information, I can see that now. Multilingual Maastrich that's what they want, Multilingual Maastricht."

Denzil Wynstanly lent back in his chair arms folded across his belly, proud of his political acumen but unaware of the inaccuracy of his comparison between Maastricht and Magna.

The interview was brought to an abrupt end with Denzil's edict." My office first thing in the morning with the initial draft. That's all Dobson, that's all."

Ned slowly made his way back to his office. His own work for that week's paper was done. Whilst the sales reps and typesetters rushed around putting the final pieces into place Dobson spent most of the day staring at a blank computer screen.

His mind floated between Denzil's ludicrous instructions for a weekly column on the Treaty of Maastricht and the merits of Sophie's exquisitely shaped bum.

By four thirty he had done nothing on the first but knew exactly what he would do if he could get his hands on the second.

It was time to call it a day. He had a five o'clock appointment at the doctors, to see if Gwendolyn's toe had left any permanent genital damage, followed by his usual two pints for the road home with Jack Prosser, in the bar of the Tip.

* * *

Jack Prosser's glass was empty and he had been drawing on his pipe for what seemed like an age waiting for Ned to continue the recounting of his visit to Doctor Lewington's surgery. There was no sign of it. Prosser suspected that Ned was beginning to slip into one of his moods and when a great cloud of regurgitated shag fumes threatened to engulf his friend his suspicions were confirmed.

"I wish you wouldn't do that Birdman." Dobson said, trying to disperse the offending cumulus with a frantic wave of his arm. "Sitting next to you is like smoking sixty fags a day. That's passive smoking that is. I could sue you for every penny you've got."

Jack Prosser ran his fingers through his mop of wiry, grey hair. He was well used to his old friend sounding off when he had a moody coming on. If it cheered him up his pal would be welcome to every one of his few pennies, and his photo album of rare British birds, and his one legged, stuffed kestrel if need be.

He took another long pull on his pipe, this time puffing the smoke through the corner of his mouth and out of harms way in deference to his pal's feelings which were obviously still a bit fragile after his accident.

It wasn't just the continual nagging pain in his crotch that was getting Dobson down, even though Lewington had assured him that there was no permanent damage and that his sex drive would return within a day or so. It was the thought of having to turn up for work in the morning fully conversant with the European Treaty of Maastricht that was the real reason for his downward moody spiral.

It was clear that Wynstanly was convinced a weekly serialisation of the Maastricht Treaty, in English and every other of Britain's multicultural languages, would put the Record back in its rightful position as the best weekly newspaper in the county. It was also clear that he, Ned Dobson, was the one lumbered with doing the job.

Eventually. "It's my shout, give us your glass," Dobson said, more out of duty than enthusiasm.

He struggled to his feet. His testes still felt like balloons after their encounter with one of Gwendolyn's size five, navy, court shoes on Friday evening. Negotiating the few paces to the bar, he gave a passable imitation of an elderly cowboy after a long day in the saddle. Sparkie Lee noted Dobson's painful progress.

"Did you get the Mother-in-Law to kiss them better?"

Sparkie shouted, trying to squeeze one more laugh out of the joke that he had milked to a standstill throughout the evening in question.

"Sod off!"

Charlie the landlord emerged from the cellar in time to give Sparkie a glare that said the fun was over and his hero's testes should be allowed to recuperate in peace.

Charlie felt partly to blame for the incident. He turned to his barmaid Rosie.

"Put Mr. Dobson's drinks on my bill." Charlie said in an effort to assuage his guilt.

"Thanks."

Rosie, the barmaid, was forty-five years of age with the figure of an athletic schoolgirl, tight, firm, desirable. Her shoulder length hair was a mass of curls and ringlets. She had a disarming, cheeky smile and the most penetrating sea green eyes Ned had ever come across. Rosie Diez was high on his list of imminent sexual conquests. Very high on his list indeed.

She delivered the two pints of best bitter courtesy of Charlie the landlord. She had a glint in her eye that was saying, 'I know where your bruises are'.

Ned noticed. "And don't you start or I'll put you over my knee my girl."

Rosie leant forward. Her face was just inches away from his. Her tight jeans, her low cut, snug fitting T-shirt, her hair dropping forward as though deliberately directing his eyes to the curves of her breasts caused Ned to be momentarily mesmerised.

"The trouble with you Ned Dobson," she whispered, "you're all talk. You know what they say don't you? – actions speak louder than words."

Her eyes were staring deep into his. His eyes were staring deep into her cleavage. In an instant she was gone. Upright, smiling and turning away to serve a customer at the other end of the bar.

Perhaps it was the pain that he was in but, for once, the man noted for his, sharp and witty, ripostes was stuck for words. He was not stuck for thoughts however and, in Ned's mind, Rosie Diez went to the top of his list, relegating the Record's Sophie to second place.

He made it back to the table without further comment from any of the regulars. Even so the Birdman was unable to prevent himself from wincing as he watched his mate slowly sit down.

"So, what was Lewington's verdict after he had examined you?"

"Got to rest them up for a bit," Dobson said resignedly.

"Give you a cushion to put in your underpants did he?" Jack said in a self-conscious effort at cheering Ned up. It failed. They spent the next ten minutes supping their beers, deep in their own contemplations.

Then, looking at his watch, Dobson said. "Ten to seven, dinner on the table in ten minutes. It's time to go."

"Yes indeed," Jack said rubbing his hands together in anticipation. "Cold beef, pickled onions and home made chips. I love Monday's grub."

"You lucky bastard," Dobson said quietly as he stared into the bottom of his glass at the last dregs of beer. "I wonder what nouvelle cuisine the old bag has got for me today."

"Er – lovely pair of willow warblers." Prosser exclaimed as they were leaving.

"What?"

"Rosie. She's got a lovely pair of willow warblers under that T-shirt"

Being more of a gentleman than Dobson, Birdman Jack Prosser would never dream of saying tits other than in an ornithological sense. It was a second attempt to cheer Ned up but it went the way of the first.

Dobson was fast sinking into one of his depressions and no amount of humorous small talk was going to bring him out of it. The mind crushing thought of having to spend the evening getting clued up on a piece of European Community clap trap not worth the paper it was written on was pushing him deeper into the pit.

Making up jokes did not come easy to Jack Prosser. When his second effort at lifting his mates' spirits failed, the Record's part time photographer gave up.

The pair walked the rest of the way up the hill from the Tip in silence. At their garden gates they bade each other the briefest of cheerios and went indoors. Dobson into No. 4 and Jack to No. 5 The Cottages, Monks End.

4

The Honey and Apple Charlotte topped with Gwendolyn's own Brandy Sauce sat majestically in the dish. Ned looked at it and it looked at Ned. It had, Ned thought, a mind, a being, a presence of its' own. It was taunting him. Daring him to ignore it and push it away uneaten. He had, until tonight, dared not. The dish, as had the previous dishes, been served by a woman who had elevated the preparation and presentation of food to a religious status. To leave one mouthful would be a sin of mortal proportions, with deadly consequences to the leaver. This resplendent pudding he was now addressing was a matter of life or death. His life or death.

Leave it uneaten and he would not feel the long handled kitchen knife until it had fully entered his back, midway between his shoulder blades. He would be instantly dispatched, expertly butchered and probably served as Beef Wellington at his own funeral.

It must be consumed, regardless of the fact that the main course of Walnut coated Lamb garnished with Broccoli and glazed Radishes had now introduced itself to the two pints of bitter taken at the Tip earlier. Ned could feel a gaseous colon evacuation of huge proportions brewing.

He sat for a moment brooding over the fact that Jack Prosser was getting stuck into cold beef and chips. Probably followed by his wife Agnes's home made gooseberry tart covered in some heavy duty custard.

Oh! for such a life of gastronomic simplicity instead of the never-ending torrent of five star à la carte that his Mother-in-Law served up day in and day out.

He was suddenly aware that the sound of silver dessert spoons against china bowls had faded. He looked up. Magenta and Gwendolyn were waiting for him to finish his dessert before coffee and optional cheese board were presented.

No. 4 The Cottages, Monks End may have once been the home of a lowly farm labourer but as long as Gwendolyn Fors-Bowers was in residence only the highest standards of etiquette and ritual would be tolerated during the evening meal. Even Dobson's headstrong and self-willed wife knew better than to take on her mother at the dinner table.

Ned studied his Mother-in-Law for a moment. She was, he thought, an alien creature floundering about in a strange world trying to survive until the rescuing spacecraft arrived to whisk her back to her natural habitat. His gaze wandered across to Magenta, who, in spite of her fondness for short skirts and low cut blouses, was growing to look more like her mother by the day. She was in the autumn of her earning days. Not even the shortest of red leather mini-skirts would do the business for a forty-something, dumpy, moustached woman.

"Just look at the pair of them." He thought. "Tweedle bleeding dum and tweedle bastard dee."

Ned's mood was deepening. Black dog was beginning to sit heavy on his shoulder. It was going to be a long, hot summer's night. He was absolutely sure that he could no longer tolerate the thought of life with these two women without the continued prospect of inheriting at least some of the family wealth.

He had paid his dues for God's sake. Put up with Gwendolyn's high and mighty attitude towards him. According to her he alone was to blame for the situation that she was in.

He had, over the years, patiently courted Randolph's favour with birthday cards, Christmas gifts and innumerable enquiries as to Randolph's general health and temper. This long running epistolary had apparently gained little ground as no hope-lifting replies were ever forthcoming.

Aching and desperate for a result Ned had played, what he regarded as, his last cards. That weekend, he had sent off two letters. One of them to Randolph Fors-Bowers. Its contents told of how: 'Randolph's daughter and grand-daughter had repented their wicked ways, turned their back on the demon drink and were now regular attendants at St. Tyllow's Church, Little Hardwicke where the Reverend Rhys Howells counted them amongst his most vigorous of worshippers. They had seen the light, signed the pledge and were constantly expounding the error and wantonness of their earlier ways. He, Randolph, could once again be proud of them. In between going to church and Women's Institute meetings they spent many hours helping the less fortunate members of the community. They were now a credit to the Fors-Bowers name and could be introduced to the most important of his neighbours with impunity.'

There was, of course, not the smallest grain of truth in any of it. The Reverend Howells had never set eyes on a Mr. Ned Dobson or his wife or Mother-in-Law. This was not only because they had never set foot inside his church but also because the vicar drank well away from both villages ensuring that his own wobbly path would not cross that of any of his parishioners.

However, the vicar had decided that he would swear certain, to anyone who should ask, that the two ladies were in his congregation every Sunday, singing the praises of the Lord and nodding approvingly at his stirring sermons. Such was the power of the financial reward promised, plus the fifty-pound note enclosed for starters, nestling in the second letter that Ned had posted.

If Ned's audacious plan worked he would be able to spend the rest of his life in clover. If it did not, if Randolph died and left them sweet bugger all, then the female occupants of 4 The Cottages, Monks End would not see his arse for dust.

"Coffee?"

Gwendolyn's voice jolted him from his daydream.

"Do – you – want – coffee?" Gwendolyn was now glowering at him from across the table.

"Not for me Mother-in-Law. I'm finished thank you."

Ned pushed the untouched dessert away from him. A brazen act unprecedented in many years of high eating at the cottage. He couldn't give a toss. He had decided that he no longer wanted to risk being cordon bleued to death. Ignoring their looks of amazement he got up from the table and went out into the garden.

It was warm. The late evening sun was just beginning to disappear behind the Cotswold hills, casting long and cooling shadows across the countryside. In the distance a blackbird was perched high in the branches of a hawthorn tree singing the praises for the end of a perfect blackbird day.

The garden also was perfect. Neat, well kept lawns. A profusion of blooming begonias, flaming fuchsias and an array of pots and hanging baskets so filled with colour that Monet himself would have been happy to spend an hour amongst them with brush and palette.

Ned also gave thanks. Not for the perfect day or his perfect garden but for the chance to release some of the accumulation of gasses that threatened an embarrassing escape at the dining table.

He farted his way down the garden path until, on reaching the garden shed, he unlocked it's door and stepped inside.

For such a well tended garden the inside of the shed showed a remarkable lack of expected implements and accessories. In fact not so much as a single item could be found therein that in any way could be regarded as useful to the enthusiastic green finger. An easy chair, a desk, a small typewriter, a television, carpeted floor and curtained windows were the unusual occupants of this particular timber and glass construction.

Those who knew Dobson well would not have to be told how this could be. They would know that digging, weeding, hoeing and planting were not any of his favourite things to do. They would know that the matriarch of the house – his mother-in-law – insisted and expected everything to be just so both inside and outside. They would also know that parting with cash to get the job done would have been just as painful as using his own sweat and moil on such a labour of hate. Finding a way to get his neighbour, Jack Prosser, to do it for free was always favourite.

The Birdman was a lover of all wildlife whether it flew or grew. He was also a dab hand with a camera and his album of rare birds was always on hand for the interested visitor.

What a stroke of luck it was for Dobson when Denzil put it around that the Record was looking for a part time photographer. A string was pulled. Prosser got the job and Dobson got a nice tidy garden plus the bonus of being able to turf out the redundant junk from his shed and turn it into a haven safe and sound from the crushing boredom of life indoors.

Even the unconventional contents of the shed had been acquired with no money changing hands. The desk, typewriter and chair were on loan from Wynstanly's refurbished office. The carpet, a radio and a television had been rescued from the local civic amenities site when there was no one watching. The television had needed repair. It also needed a supply of electricity. Both jobs were expertly completed by Sparky in return for the draft of a speech for his daughter's upcoming wedding.

It had crossed Ned's mind on more than one occasion that organising this garden bolthole was one of his more sensible moves.

He sank into the chair and put his feet up on the desk. From this position he was able to unlock the bottom draw and take out one of a dozen or more cans of bitter that were stashed inside. He tuned the radio into the Monday night jazz programme. Woody Herman was 'Jumping at the Savoy'. Ned set about wiping out those brain cells that held the memories of a bad day.

Eventually the late evening sunlight that had once filled his refuge gave way to the shadows of a warm July night.

Ned did not notice. If the massed bands of the Coldstream Guards had clashed with a crowd of rioting new age travellers, Ned would not have noticed. He was now into his ninth can and had sunk deep into his own private world. Deep down inside one of his quiet spells.

When the banality of his life hit him hard and became more of a bitch than usual his tried and tested remedy was to surrender, belly up, in total capitulation. Fighting back took energy. Drowning in a pottage of despair and a belly full of strong ale was far more acceptable and fast becoming one of the highlights of his life. A Ned Dobson quiet spell could last for a couple of hours or drag on for a couple of days. It really wasn't up to him. He had no control over the matter. The motivation to rejoin the rat race inevitably had to come from an outside source. On this occasion the motivation was going to come from his boss, Denzil Wynstanly, first thing in the morning.

Ned was aware of the impending confrontation but was not bothered by it. A copy of the Maastricht Treaty, culled from one of the more up market Sunday papers, remained in the top drawer of the desk untouched. He had no intention of trying to make any sense of this load of European rubbish. Not for Wynstanly or anyone.

In the still of the night his thoughts turned to Rosie. He could see her smiling face just inches from his. He fancied her like hell. He was missing her like hell. Ella Fitzgerald sang 'Every time we say goodbye, I die a little –'. He ring pulled another can of beer, his tenth, and took a long, deep pull on it.

* * *

Jack Prosser was taking his usual late night stroll

around his own garden. The Cottages backed on to Jake Brown's Hill Farm. As usual there were plenty of night sounds for him to cock an ear to. He had already heard an owl. A couple of hedgehogs were snuffling about for their evening meal and, somewhere in the distance, a fox was barking. He could also hear the sound of someone snoring. It seemed to be coming from Dobson's shed. Maybe not. Night sounds came sometimes play tricks on old ears. He decided that it was time to turn in.

5

At the very moment that Dobson had entered his shed and commenced his moody decent into alcoholic oblivion Denzil Wynstanly was on the golf course, down on his haunches, surveying what was about to become a winning put. His partner, Frankie Ferranti, had left him with a difficult fourteen footer. Up and over a ridge with a faint left hand borrow. If he sank it the match would be theirs.

It was a situation likely to turn many an iron willed and confident golfer into a gibbering heap. But this vital and crucial moment held no terrors for Wynstanly. He felt good. He felt very good. He had played immaculate golf all evening. Out of trees, out of rough, out of bunkers. In fact, wherever his wayward and edgy partner had deemed to leave the ball he, Denzil Wynstanly, was more than equal to it.

"What do you think Frankie? Slight breeze head on. Green still a bit rubbery from the weekend shower?" Denzil asked.

Frankie Ferranti offered no comment. He was praying to as many saints as he could think of to come down and spirit the ball into the hole so that he could get off the course and away from the club as fast as his waxed Italian legs could carry him.

Wynstanly settled himself down and addressed the ball.

"This for a place in the final." He murmured and slowly swung his putter back.

Vaughan Ames and Chief Inspector Touber stood a polite and respectful distance away close to the edge of the green. A bemused Ames simply could not understand how he and the Chief Inspector could be on the verge of being beaten three and two by a couple of no hopers. A scratch pairing of that fool Wynstanly and a night-club owner about whom little was known except that he was no great golfer. The events of the evening's match were hardly credible. He had not seen Wynstanly so up beat and cocksure of himself for months. There was something up, Ames was certain of that, but he could not decide what it was.

His suspicions were first aroused when they walked off the tenth green all square. By rights the match should have been settled there and then, given the superiority of his and Touber's golf. But Wynstanly was playing out of his skin. Playing amazingly well and with great confidence for someone who was supposed to be under the community cosh with his newspaper struggling and trailing in the popularity stakes. Whilst Denzil was on top form his partner, Ferranti, was not only out of it but behaving in a most peculiar manner.

Frankie Ferranti, owner of the Blue Lagoon nightclub, was not from one of the many Italo-British families who had happily settled in the country. Many excellent chip shops and coffee bars would not exist without the Sidoli's and the Rabioti's of the British Isles

Ferranti was not one of this band of popular immigrants. He was a loner. A one off who had suddenly appeared to rescue the ailing Blue Lagoon club which was situated midway between Gloucester and Cheltenham.

Almost overnight he had turned the Lagoon into the place to go. Instantly he became a popular purveyor of good times with the clubbers. His free bus service ensured that his club was always buzzing with people – buzzing. The Lagoon now went a long way towards satisfying the famously insatiable appetites of the Gloucestershire pleasure seekers. Every night was party night and every night someone in Gloucestershire wanted to party.

Having made it with the in crowd Frankie set about courting a more discernible form of respectability. Joining the Wold Golf and Country club was a step towards masking his more sinister activities.

His sudden appearance and the sharp rise in the fortunes of the Blue Lagoon Night Spot had not gone unnoticed by the local police.

"Where," they asked "has this, Italian gentleman in his late twenties come from?"

"How," they mused "did he acquire the money to buy and re-equip the Lagoon?"

They sought the answer to these and other questions but Frankie was sharper than his hand made Italian suits. Too clever for the Detective Constables and Detective Inspectors who often beat a, size nine, path to his door in the hope of finding the answers.

One of the causes of Frankie's edginess on the golf course, that evening, was Chief Inspector Touber, Ames' golfing partner. Ferranti could handle the middle and upper ranks but a Chief Inspector was a whole new policeman's ball game. A chief had a nose for villains. A chief could smell villains through a nose blocked with crusted snot. The other cause of his edginess was the pick me up he had indulged in that afternoon. It was beginning to wear off.

When Frankie had learned that it would be Touber who would be walking the course with him his heart had sunk lower that the Italian Lire when set against the Deutschmark. He had, that very evening, committed himself to a bit of business at the club which was impossible for him to put off.

When Denzil and Frankie went one up at the twelfth Ames gave serious consideration to the possibility that the shady Ferranti had supplied Wynstanly with some illegal performance enhancing substance. When Wynstanly holed the fourteenth with a bunker shot from thirty metres Vaughan Ames came within a whisker of suggesting to Touber that he radio ahead for drug squad officers and sniffer dogs.

Had Ames carried out his intentions and the clubhouse was seen to be surrounded with flashing blue lights, Frankie Ferranti would have filled his silk designer boxer shorts with a large amount of bodily waste matter.

Denzil's putter made perfect connection. The ball reached the top of the ridge then charged down the slope like the rescuing cavalry in a Randolph Scott movie. It curved to the left before making a satisfying plop as it hit the bottom of the cup.

He flung his arms in the air. Victory was his. Victory over Ames tonight and again tomorrow and tomorrow and tomorrow. With his man Dobson working on the Records' serialisation of the Maastricht Treaty – in English and all the others of course – he was going to be a local hero once again.

"Very well played Denzil," Chief Inspector Touber was the first to congratulate him. "And good luck in the final on Saturday."

"An interesting game Denzil. I hope your luck holds out until the weekend," said Ames.

"Thank you Vaughan. I'm sure it will. In fact I have a feeling that I am going to be on top of the game for quite a while – quite a long while".

Wynstanly ignored Ames's quizzical look and turned to pat his partner on the back. But Frankie was nowhere to be seen. He was already back at the clubhouse.

Frankie ran into the locker room. With golf bag over his shoulder he fumbled in his trouser pocket, took out a key and unlocked the door. His hand trembled as he opened it. Inside was a large black and red sports bag identical to the one he had brought to the club earlier. He took it out and slammed the door shut. As he was hurrying through reception he heard his name being called.

"Mr. Ferranti – Mr. Ferranti there's a call for you". The receptionist was holding out a telephone. "Would you like to take it here?"

Frankie took the receiver and waited until she had moved away.

"Hello – Ferranti speaking".

"Frankie – my dear old thing I'm so glad I caught

you. Were you just on your way out? I hear your golf match was a resounding success. I do believe we have a budding Ballesteros in our midst. Oh! dear me what am I saying? He is a Spaniard is he not? It seems that the world is still waiting for its first Italian Master. One day dear boy. One day."

Frankie recognised the voice instantly. He could not put a name to it for it had never been offered to him. Neither could he put a face to it for he had never seen it. It could have been the voice of the perfect English gentleman except that the man behind it, although a perfectionist, was in no way a gentleman. Of that Frankie was well aware. He did not attempt to engage The Voice in any form of conversation. His duty was to wait and listen to the purpose of the call. And while he waited he wondered how The Voice already knew the result of the match that had finished only moments ago.

"Frankie, my dear sweet potato, my salesman in Amsterdam has lost a complete set of samples. Now isn't that just too careless of him? And whilst on his way to a most important client. I really must slap his wrist the very next time that I see him. Be an angel and meet me in the a.m. at the usual. Ciau dear boy – ciau."

Frankie Ferranti sighed as he replaced the receiver.

"Mama mia!" He raised his eyes to the heavens. "Why always me – why?"

The sight of Chief Inspector Touber striding off the golf course convinced Frankie that he should not hang around for any celestial reply to his question. He exited the Wold Golf and Country Club pretty damned quickly. Golf bag over one shoulder and a sports bag containing twenty-five pounds of pure Colombian cocaine over the other.

6

"Help! – help! – somebody help – wake up you stupid women – anybody – help! – help!"

Ned had been shouting for, what seemed to him like, an eternity. His desperate cries and vehement curses had not born fruit. That is to say they had failed to attract the attention of any fellow human being willing to come forward and extract him from his disagreeable and uncomfortable predicament.

"Help! – somebody come and get me out of here," he shouted.

"Help! get a doctor – get an ambulance – get a bloody crane – I can't move – I can't bloody well move."

Ned Dobson had one of those confounding constitutions that irritated his fellow drinkers. Many a drinking companion would part company with him after a particularly heavy session fully believing that he (Dobson) would never walk, or talk properly, ever again. Only to be proved wrong when Dobson would emerge bright and early the following morning eager for a repeat performance. He also had a remarkable body clock. Without fail it would wake him at fifteen minutes past seven every morning, inexplicably adjusting itself to the to-ing and fro-ing of British summer and winter times with no obvious mechanical aid from the likes of an alarm clock.

It woke him at fifteen minutes past seven this bright July morning as usual. His head felt none the worse for the twelve cans of beer that he had seen off the previous evening. He had woken up to discover that he was still in the shed. Still sat in the chair with his feet up on the desk. At least, they looked like his feet. They were his shoes all right and definitely his trousers but whether the contents belonged to him he had no way of telling for he had no feeling from his waist downwards. No feeling, no movement, no control. It felt as though he had been super-glued to chair and desk in the dead of night by some ghoulish prankster. A revenge driven husband? A jealous boyfriend? Hardly likely. If such persons had discovered Dobson immobile and helpless they would not have let the opportunity to remove his external genitalia pass by unfulfilled. He would have woken to find his willy dangling before his eyes and pointing at him accusingly. No indeed, his, almost total, seizure was entirely down to his own foolishness. He had spent the night in a most inadvisable position, feet and legs angled sharply upwards with a draught coming in from the open window. A stiff neck accompanied his lower numbness, but the ache in his neck and shoulders proved that at least part of him was still alive.

"Prosser, you bastard – get your arse down here – I'm stuck – can't move a bloody inch – HELP! – HELP! – you bastards HELP!"

The window in Dobson's shed opened out in the direction of Jake Brown's fields. Jake's sheep had heard everything but understood nothing. Sheep are not known for the hugeness of their I.Q. Indeed it is known throughout the educated world that sheep have only three purposes in their grass chewing lives – to provide food – to provide wool – and newcomers to the third are always advised to wear a large pair of wellingtons.

Gwendolyn looked at her watch. It was twenty minutes past eight. She occupied the back bedroom of No. 4 the Cottages and had heard Dobson calling. Heard him, in fact, almost as soon as he had started his appeals for assistance more than an hour earlier.

Had she come from the lower classes she would have slipped on her dressing gown and stepped out to see what all the fuss was about. Instead she had bathed, dressed, brushed her hair, applied make up and was now ready to risk being seen by the neighbours. She arrived at the shed window impeccably turned out.

"About bloody time. Where have you been? Didn't you hear me shouting? Are you deaf or what?" There was a marked lack of respect in Dobson's tone. Having inflicted the supreme insult on Gwendolyn by refusing her Honey and Apple Charlotte the previous evening, paying her respect now seemed a pointless exercise.

"Look, I've locked the door. The keys are there on the desk – reach your fat arm through the window and get them – just get me out of here – I can't move – get me out – I'll be late for work."

Gwendolyn stared at the keys and then at him. Without a word she disappeared from his view.

"Hey! you stupid cow. Get back here – where do you think you are going? I've got to get to work – Wynstanly will have my balls for breakfast."

Gwendolyn reappeared a moment later carrying a broom. Her original intention was to hook the keys towards the window unlock the door and let him out. That however would mean her having to lift his legs off the desk, to touch him. She changed her mind, realising that once circulation had been restored he would be able to fend for himself. She pushed the broom through the open window and positioned the brush head against his chest.

"Hey! – Hey! What do you think you are doing? Hey! – steady on – steady on". A look of concern appeared on Dobson's face.

Gwendolyn gave a mighty push.

"Arragh –!" Dobson could only manage a strangled shout of fear and surprise before he was tipped arse over head. As his feet passed through the one hundred and eightieth degree his glasses departed from his face and he crashed on to the floor face down with the chair on top of him.

Gwendolyn allowed herself the smallest of smiles at a job well done and returned to the house to prepare breakfast leaving her surly son-in-law on the floor of the shed vigorously encouraging a supply of blood to re-occupy his drained legs and feet.

* * *

Whilst Dobson was stumbling out of his shed trying to remember how to walk Frankie Ferranti was driving his red Alfa Romeo towards the old Severn Bridge heading for the service station at Aust. The spell of warm weather showed no sign of ending. It was eight thirty and the morning sun had been up for three hours or more. Frankie had been up all night. When the last of his staff had left the Lagoon at 3 a.m. he had gone to his rooms and watched a video.

Frankie often stayed awake. Sleeping was a wasteful pastime. He needed little of it especially since he had started sampling some of the company's excellent products. Yes, he knew the dangers. Dealing and using was a dangerous combination. Enrico had warned him before he left Florence.

"Listen to me Frankie. The U.K. branch is run by a ruthless man. He will not tolerate inefficiency. Remember what happened to Louis and keep your nose clean." Enrico's final and pointed remark was accompanied with two gentle slaps on the face.

Frankie remembered Louis, his predecessor. A rising star destined for big success. If he had continued to prove himself and kept his head Louis would have been moved on to Europe and eventually to America as boss of his own unit.

Louis lost his head. The Voice had arranged for it to be separated from his body and sent on a world tour in the hold of a Jumbo jet.

But Louis was a fool. He failed to control his habit. HE, Frankie Ferranti, was in command. Besides, was not staying awake and dealing of more benefit to the company than lying asleep in bed? He would not make the same mistake as Louis. He would get himself a wife. A nice Italian girl who would look after him.

Oh! he had no complaints with British girls. Most of the countries national females had visited his club. Welsh girls in particular were sensuous, fiery and very,

very passionate. He had heard of Welsh 'hywl' but after a marathon session with one visiting black haired and vigorous Welsh nymph, had decided that the word was wasted on the national sport of rugby. His own dark Latin looks and seemingly endless supply of money guaranteed him as many of these bedroom conversions as he could handle. But an Italian girl it would have to be. One who understood and knew how to behave with his business acquaintances.

He turned off the motorway just before the bridge. As he drove up the long approach road to the services car park he decided that when this bit of business with The Voice had been concluded he would take a few days holiday in his home town of Florence. A pretty Italian wife would add one more notch on to his totem of respectability.

Frankie drove down to the far end of the parking area and nosed the car into one of the bays. He immediately got out and went to the rear where he opened the boot and took out a small folding canvas chair. He opened the chair and placed it on the grass so that he sat facing the Bristol Channel thus ensuring that his back was turned to any incoming vehicles. He hardly had time to open his copy of the morning's Financial Times when he heard the soft purring of a large and expensive car. A black limousine reversed into the bay next to Frankie's and stopped. Frankie knew that he must not look round. The Voice had arrived.

The Voice had a minder, Brian. A short man by minder standards, five feet six, but incredibly wide. It had crossed Frankie's mind the first time he saw Brian that if the man were to lay on his side he would still reach five feet six. Bulging biceps, calves, thighs and pectorals pushed and jostled under the man's close fitting double breasted grey suit indicating to Frankie that Brian must have been pumping more than iron to arrive at such a physique.

His very first sighting of Brian, the steroid, with chauffeur's cap perched on boulder like head had caused Frankie to smile. The look that Brian had given him in return encouraged Frankie to remember never to smile in that man's company again.

He heard Brian get out of the car. A dark shadow was cast around Frankie's chair as the minder took up his position in front of him. From a distance it would appear that the pair were engaged in innocuous conversation. Brian glanced around the car park before nodding in the direction of the limousine – a signal that all was well.

At these meetings The Voice never got out of the car. His lightly talcumed Armani covered backside remained seated on the plush leather upholstery. The rear window was lowered just enough for Frankie to hear what was to be said and just enough for him to get a whiff of Guy Laroche perfume.

"Frankie! Frankie! so nice to see you again dear boy – and always so punctual. I knew you would not keep me waiting. I mused that very thing not moments ago. 'Mr. Ferranti will not keep us waiting' were the very words themselves is that not so Brian?"

Brian the steroid nodded his head in agreement.

The Voice went on. "I always maintain that if the appointed time was deemed to be mutually agreeable then it is nothing less than good manners for it to be mutually met. I am a veritable slave to punctuality and, dear heart, expect nothing less from my men. A tardy employee is a hurtful employee, don't you agree Francesco? And you have no idea how much Brian hates to see me hurt. He is SO protective – he would do ANYTHING to ensure that I am never kept waiting. It is such a comfort."

Brian pushed his box like chest out to its utmost extremity on hearing his masters accolade. Frankie Ferranti had not put a foot wrong in the prelude to this meeting. He had been on time as usual, had set out the canvas chair in the correct manner, was properly suited and tied with a deep shine on his shoes. Yet by intimating that Brain would inflict hurt and excruciating pain on him had he been just one minute late The Voice had skilfully manoeuvred him into servile position "A".

"So, how goes it with you Frankie? How fortunate you are to work in such a beautiful part of the country. The rolling Wiltshire countryside, the gentle folds of the Cotswolds, and so close to Wales too. Another beautiful part of the country I'm told – Look! I can see it from here. Those hills – such majestic hills. Is it no wonder that the Welsh have such powerful lungs if they have to negotiate such perpendicular topography? And the girls – Ah! Frankie I hear of the Welsh girls. Black eyed vixens who think nought of clawing the flesh of a man's back at their point of climax – a touch over exuberant for my taste but, c'est la vie – vive la femme. Oh! there I go again slipping into a little French when I should be slipping into a little Italian."

Brian's huge shoulders began to shake. He had spotted one of his master's jokes. Ferranti thought it too much to hope for that it was the one about perpendicular topography. More likely to be the one where he, Brian, holds the greasy little Itie in a headlock while his master gives him, Frankie, a good rogering. The Voice also must know of his recent romantic liaison with the Welsh girl. How does he do it?

"But to business my aubergine, my sweet treaded grape, to business. I gently flambéed the Amsterdam problem with you on the telephone yesterday. Sadly, overnight, I was forced to turn up the heat and our man in Amsterdam is now – shall we say – well done. It has left me with a problem. And who do I turn to when I have a problem? Who's name is forever on my lips when my brow is furrowed and troubled? Who Frankie? – WHO?"

Frankie did not have to be told who. He bloody well knew who. It was effing Frankie Ferranti that's who.

The Voice lowered his tone. From now on there would be no more small talk. No more fannying about, this was what Frankie had been summoned to hear.

51

"One of my most important clients, a much travelled man, a worldly man, missed his Amsterdam pick up last week, due to our late employee's incompetence. I have no need to tell you what a great source of embarrassment that was to me. Fortunately for all of us he will be in Copenhagen on Thursday of this week and I want you, my dear Frankie to ensure that he receives one whole kilo of our very best and immaculate product – without fail."

"You mean THIS Thursday? – but that's –"

"Two whole days away Frankie – two whole days. A man of your connections, of your charm, of your – persuasiveness should have the merest of problems finding a willing courier. I need not remind you that you are being watched and to attempt to carry out this operation yourself would be an act of pure folly with potentially dangerous consequences."

The Voice paused, but more for effect than in anticipation of another interruption.

"This Thursday evening at precisely nineteen hundred hours Central European Time, a man will be waiting in Copenhagen's Tivoli Gardens. Your courier will find him among the crowd in front of the bandstand, to the right of the Balkan restaurant. He will be wearing a light grey suit and a black T-shirt, on which will be printed the words The Copenhagen Connection – so often it is the obvious that goes completely unnoticed. The Copenhagen Connection will have with him a blue and white S.A.S. flight bag, identical to the one that Brian will hand you a moment from now and into which you will secrete the product in any way you think fit. The bags will be exchanged and you will deliver the Danish bag, which will contain 100,000 pounds sterling, to me personally at this very spot one week from today. I know that this is not our normal way of operating but I am in a difficult and sensitive situation and risks have to be taken. I am confident that you, my dear Frankie, will not let me down."

The rear window of the limousine closed and Brian

walked to the car. He returned and placed a Scandinavian Airlines System flight bag at Frankie's feet. As Frankie picked it up the black limousine drove away.

7

At fifteen minutes past nine Frankie Ferranti was leaving the Old Severn Bridge behind him and heading for the M5 and Cheltenham. Frankie was concerned. The Voice's words 'we must take risks' were running around unchecked inside his head.

"WE must take risks? It is me Frankie who is taking the risk," he thought. "I am the one who has to find a courier. I am the one who they will come looking for if this crazy plan goes wrong". He was beginning to feel tired. He drove a mile passed the next junction and pulled over on to the hard shoulder. He removed what looked like a cigarette lighter from the dashboard. His briefcase was lying on the passenger seat of his car. Clicking the top of the lighter he quickly laid out a thin line of white powder along the side of the case. He rolled a twenty pound note into a thin tube and in a moment the powder disappeared from the case and into his nose and respiratory system. Wetting the end of his fore finger with his tongue he dabbed up the residue and licked his finger clean.

He drove on and in a few moments felt supremely confident that he would easily find some idiot to carry out this simplest of tasks in the Danish capital.

At the same time Ned Dobson was hurrying along Gloucester's Eastgate Street. He was, not surprisingly, late for work. No one was ever late for work at the Record. Today Dobson was not only late but he had prepared nothing on the Maastricht Treaty. Wynstanly would have his, already bruised, testes on a spit and he could see his P45 looming large before his eyes.

At the Record it is Tuesday mornings not Monday mornings that are flat and difficult to get into. Monday is print day. The day when the paper finally appears in all its tabloid glory and begins its long journey to the towns and villages throughout the County.

So it is that Tuesdays become Mondays and Monday morning blues do not commence until Tuesday morning – such is the strange and twilight world of the local, weekly, newspaper business.

However, this Tuesday morning, at the Record's offices, there was an unusual and unfamiliar air of joyfulness about the place. It started when Denzil greeted Sophie with a cheerie good morning instead of his customary grunt and surly demand for his first cup of coffee.

It progressed as he repeated this greeting to each of the studio staff in turn and by name. And it reached an all time high when he congratulated both the Sales Manager and the Editor on a fine paper even though advertising revenue was barely covering costs and editorial content was weaker than a bowl of fresh air soup.

Neither the Sales Manager nor the Editor could offer an explanation for Wynstanly's good humour and their confusion deepened when all three spotted Dobson puffing along the street his collar and tie in disarray, his shirt hanging out of the front of his trousers and – his glasses? – The bridge and right arm looked to be held together with green insulation tape and the right hand lens seemed to be missing completely.

"Oh! the poor chap," said Denzil. "He's been working too hard. I must insist he takes a few days off."

The Sales Manager and the Editor looked at each other, both searching for a sign of understanding on the other's face. As Dobson passed through reception Sophie called out to him from her office.

"He's rang down for you twice already. He is very excited about something."

"Thanks Soph." Ned passed her office door without giving her a glance. His usual morning ritual of fuelling up on her desirable body would set his loins up for the day. His loins would have to wait. He had a head to head with D.W. to get over with and the previous nights defiant attitude was now leaking out of every pore. By the time he was at the top of the stairs and standing outside Denzil's office he was drained of every fluid ounce and stood there flaccidly awaiting his fate.

With his head bowed, as a condemned man would indicate his readiness for the drop, he knocked on the door.

"Come in Edward. Come in."

Ned paused. Denzil had never, ever, called him by his first name. He opened the door and went in.

"Good heavens, Edward. Look at the state of you. I know I set you a bit of a task but I didn't expect you to be at it all night. Sit down old chap. Sit down." Denzil picked up his internal telephone.

"Sophie – two cups of coffee please and quickly if you would. Edward looks as though he could do with one."

Ned smiled, sheepishly.

"Now then Edward, what have you got for me? A plan of action I hope. A masterful way to present the Maastricht Treaty to our eager public? Something sharp, concise, readable and interesting?"

It was an excited and sweating Denzil Wynstanly who reeled off a stream of adjectives which Ned regarded as being not remotely connected to the document in question. When he had finished his reeling Wynstanly noticed that Dobson was squinting at him through one lens.

"Edward, what has happened to your glasses?"

"Er – well –."

"No matter – first things first. Off you go then. The quicker we get started the quicker Vaughan Ames and his Clarion get dumped into the Bristol Channel. Let's hear it then man. Spit it out. You've no idea how much I have been waiting for this moment." Denzil rubbed his fat sweaty hands together in anticipation.

Wynstanly's charm and affability left Ned bewildered. If his boss had been his usual grouchy self this morning he would have known how to handle him. A little grovelling, some forelock touching and a quick scuttle out of his office with a quick "it won't happen again sir" and it would have been over and done with. But this smiling, happy and excited man in front of him was a stranger.

What could he say to him? What the bloody hell could he say to him?. Should he tell him the truth? That he thought a wet fart would stick to a pair of 'Y'-fronts closer than the countries of Europe would bond. That, at the first sign of any real trouble the whole, overblown, bureaucratic lot would disappear down the pan quicker than the waste matter from a double vindaloo? That the Maastricht Treaty was a load of old bollocks? A bollock lake? A bollock mountain? The biggest load of bollocky bollocks ever cobbled together by a bunch of dithering old pillocks with no bollocks? What the bloody hell was he going to say to him?

"Well Sir – the thing is – this Treaty – well Sir –."

"Edward! Edward!" Denzil interrupted. "Not Sir – not you and I – together – you know – been through hell and high water. So when it's you and I – together – it's Denzil. OK?"

Ned nodded. "Yes er Den – Den – er Denzil. Whatever you say."

There was no obvious sign that his boss had gone mad but that was not proof enough. Ned had always maintained that the dividing line between sanity and lunacy was a very thin one indeed.

After all, Denzil really believed that his readers would be beside themselves with joy when they discovered that his paper was publishing a weekly serialisation of the Maastricht Treaty – in English and sundry other languages. Men had been certified for less.

Denzil, if not already completely round the bend, could be teetering on the very edge of insanity. If he, Ned, could not find a way to keep his boss calm and happy he had visions of the ivory handled letter opener that was lying close to Denzils right hand being plunged at his groin. Nailing his dick to the very seat that he was

57

sat in. A dick with more than one hole in it, although bound to have great curiosity value both with past and future sexual conquests, did not appeal to him.

For a brief moment Ned bent his head in silent prayer. Slowly bits of a conversation between himself, Prosser, Jake Brown, Sparky Lee and Charlie the Landlord began emerging from the recesses of his mind. He remembered how, on a warm July evening in 1992, they cheered and shouted at the bar room television urging the Danish football team to victory in the European Cup Final. And how, after the Danes had lifted the cup and the excitement and euphoria had settled down, he remembered how they remembered that Denmark had not even qualified for the tournament in the first place.

Ned gathered up those thoughts that were floating around in his mind and with a little journalistic licence quickly added a few thoughts of his own. When mixed together they created an intriguing and potent cocktail.

"The thing is Denzil there is something very odd about this whole Maastricht thing. Something very odd indeed."

"Odd? In what way odd?"

"I've got these informants."

"Informants Edward?"

"Yes, sources of international information. They tell me that news is just now leaking out that the second Danish referendum and the subsequent yes vote in favour of the Treaty was arrived at – well – not quite in the usual and legal way."

Ned was aware that he had now started something but was not sure where it was going or where it would end up.

But Denzils curiosity was aroused. He leaned forward. "What do you mean not in the usual way? Are you saying that the Danish referendum on Maastricht was – was – illegal?"

The word sounded preposterous.

Ned continued. "My informants laid some interesting

facts in front of me in the early hours of this morning. Facts connecting the result of the European Cup Final and the Danes voting on Maastricht. Facts which if proved correct will blow the lid off the biggest can of European worms ever and send the whole house of cards flying about like autumn leaves in a gale force wind."

Suddenly Denzil's eyes lit up like twin bonfires. Just as he believed that he was a great salesman so he also believed that he was a great newspaper man, with an instinct for a big story. This unreliable instinct began to take over from the incredulous feeling that he had a moment ago. A shiver of excitement passed through his huge body. He reached further forward grasping Dobson's hands in his, pulling him towards him until their faces were almost touching. He was sure that Dobson had stumbled onto a major international scandal and he could hardly contain himself in the anticipation of what was coming next.

What came next were two cups of coffee, on a tray, brought in by Sophie. She had just left the lower office where Spike was organising an office sweep stake. A childish but necessary interlude in the daily grind. Spike was asking for the most imaginative reason for Wynstanly's unexpected good mood this morning. Entries were a pound each and the one judged to be the winner collected the kitty.

Downstairs in the lower office imaginations were running riot.

The sight of her Managing Director and Mr. Dobson (Edward as her boss had called him) holding hands and apparently gazing deeply into each other's eyes phased Sophie for a moment. She walked over to the desk and placed the cups of coffee down. As she did so she realised that the sugar bowl was missing.

"Oh! sorry. I've forgotten the sugar Mr. Wynstanly. I'll be right back".

Neither one of them paid any attention to her. Both men's eyes were locked together. She stifled a gasp. Had she stumbled across the real reason for Mr. Wystanly's good humour this morning?

Was he? – was? – were he and Mr. Dobson? – had they fallen in? – were they? ...

The complete sentence just would not come together in her mind but there was no denying it. There was every indication that she was looking at two men who were – WHO WERE IN LOVE!!!.

There, she had thought the unthinkable but it looked so obviously right that it must be true. She tiptoed out of the room.

"Well?"

"Well?"

"What's the connection Edward?" Denzil said excitedly. Blobs of sweat were beginning to fall from his flabby jowls onto his sweat stained desk. He had already made the connection even before Ned had finished inventing it.

"Connection?"

"Between the Danes winning the cup and their referendum on the Treaty." Wynstanly was fidgeting in his chair. Its tanned leather seat was slippery with wetness. "Tell me Edward. Tell me what you have heard from Europe. Speak man, you look as though you are in a trance."

Whilst the two had been staring at each other Ned had been putting the final touches to what he thought was a most ludicrous suggestion. Unknown to him Wynstanly was not only one jump ahead of him but had put two and two together to make six and had crossed the T's and dotted the I's on the same ludicrous bag of bones.

"Well," said Ned, "Denmark – the footballing Denmark that is – failed to qualify for the European finals in 1992."

"And yet they became the European Champions." Denzil exclaimed emphatically.

"Yes. They got into the finals by replacing Yugoslavia who could not compete because of the war. So

Denmark were called up at the last minute to make up the numbers so to speak. They had no time to prepare like the rest of the teams. No lounging around hotel swimming pools being waited on hand foot and finger. These lads were dragged in from their holidays, their gardening or doing the washing up just days before their first game at the Malmo stadium against England who, at the time, fancied their chances of at least getting to the semis".

"And the result was –?"

"A nil – nil draw. A bit of a shock result it was really."

"Of course it was," Denzil said knowingly. "Of course it was."

"Well there were more shock results to come. The Danes turned over Germany."

"Who also fancied their chances," Denzil interrupted, his voice rising with excitement.

"Absolutely. Then the Danes got to the final in Gothenburg and beat Holland who not only fancied their chances but were the red hot favourites for the whole show. A bit of a fairy tale ending really."

"Indeed Edward. A fairy tale ending the likes of which Hans Christian Anderson would have been proud of – he, also, was a Dane you know. Now, draw me your conclusions Edward. Draw me your conclusions." Denzil repeated with obvious joy.

"Well –." Ned eyed Denzil suspiciously. He could see that he had managed to keep his boss happy by the expressions on his face but had failed completely to keep him calm as Denzil was fidgeting about in his chair like a kid who had just weed itself and he was grasping Ned's hand even more tightly than before.

"Well –." Ned started again. this time he tried to release Denzils grip. If the boss was going to flip his lid then he felt it imperative that he should be able to make a quick exit. He failed. Denzil was not going to let go. "You see the month before the Championships, Denmark – the country that is – held a referendum on the

61

Treaty of Maastricht and registered a NO vote. And this NO looked like upsetting the European apple cart."

"I remember! I remember it well," Denzil confirmed.

"Then, and this is the tricky bit, as soon as they get their hands on the cup they –."

Denzil jumped in. "They hold another referendum and vote YES. YES! YES! YES! They voted YES. The football team gets the cup provided Maastricht got a YES at the second referendum. The whole thing was a fix Edward. A huge fix." Denzil's face was now covered in sweat. Even the palms of his hands were sweating. Ned could feel Denzil's perspiration running between his own fingers.

"Was it?" Ned said. Beginning to finding his own incredulous story incredulous.

"Yes Edward, and you are the one who has uncovered it."

"Have I?"

"Well done Edward. Very well done". And an excited Denzil Wynstanly banged Ned's hand up and down on the desk.

"Yes! But it's just leaks and rumours." Ned said, trying to water down the issue. "Nothing concrete. Just leaks and rumours."

"But don't you see Edward, it all adds up. How many referendums have we had in this country in the past thirty years?"

"Well we've had – um – er – not many – hardly more than er –."

"ONE! Edward. Just one in thirty years. Referendums are costly and time consuming and critics say that the questions can be worded ambiguously making the results inconclusive. We have one in thirty years the Danes have two in almost as many months. Doesn't that strike you as more than bit suspicious?"

"Well – yes but a fix?" Ned tried again to drag his hand away from Denzils sweaty palms but failed. "I mean to say every Government in Europe would have to be in on it wouldn't they? That's hardly likely is it?" The tables had now been turned. What started out as a little, white, journalistic lie to get him off Denzil's hook now had him wriggling and squirming. And the more he wriggled and squirmed the more hooked he became.

"Edward, do you think that it is 'hardly likely' that the more powerful European Governments would not go to any means to keep the Union intact?"

"Yes, but – well what about the football players? You'd never get all of them to –.'

"But don't you see? You would not need all of them. Just a few who are not adverse to earning a little extra. Even I am aware that international goalkeepers have been known to, inexplicably, dive over a ball allowing it to slip into the net."

"Yes, but – what about the officials, the managers, the television cameras? The eyes of the footballing world were watching. I can't see how it could have been done." Ned protested, quite forgetting that the whole story was his idea in the first place.

"Edward, Edward, Edward." Ned's hand was being banged down on the desk at each mention of his name. "When Governments want something for their own ends they will stop at nothing – not even murder – to get it. They have ways, unstoppable ways, crushing ways of achieving their aims. Trust me Edward I am a newspaper man. There is a huge story here and you are going to Copenhagen to root it out. Congratulations Edward, congratulations."

Denzil stood up and, dragging Ned with him, placed one of his sweaty hands behind Ned's neck, pulled him across the desk and was in the process of giving him a big hug just as Sophie returned with the sugar.

Downstairs, Spike's sweep-stake had attracted some extreme and fatuous replies. Entries for the 'why is Denzil as chuffed as buggery' competition included: The Clarion's offices had been gutted by a mysterious fire during the night; Vaughan Ames had been caught soliciting in a Cheltenham public convenience; Denzil's one and only premium bond purchased in 1964 for one pound had just won him a million quid.

Back in her office, Sophie was hesitating as she pondered the merits of her own extreme and fatuous entry when her telephone rang. It was her Managing Director. "Sophie, would you get on to the travel agents straight away and book two seats on to the first available flight to Copenhagen. Call me with the details as soon as you can."

Sophie needed no more convincing. Her employer and Mr. Dobson were off to the Danish capital for a dirty weekend together. She wrote out her entry and was about to take it to the sales manager when the telephone rang again.

"Sophie, I quite forgot to mention that you must book one ticket for Mr. Dobson and the other one for Mr. Jack Prosser the photographer."

She quickly slipped her potentially libellous answer into her handbag and set about thinking up another one.

8

The offices of the Clarion were situated at the far end of Westgate Street just a quarter of a mile from the Record. Vaughan Ames was standing at his ground floor window watching the last minute shoppers scurrying about making their purchases. The incessant flow of traffic was beginning to ease and the day time activities of the town were winding down in readiness for the vibrant and vibrating night life to swing into action.

In a few hours time the area would be jumping. Even though it was still only Tuesday its taverns and clubs would be bursting at the seams. Throbbing and gyrating with seekers of the ultimate pleasures. Countless Bang and Olufsen systems, close to the limits of their capabilities, would soon be pumping out mega quantities of decibels of repetitive disco music that would force its way up into the evening sky. The complete and absolute deterrent to would be raiders from another galaxy and probably the reason why UFO's never stay around long enough to be identified.

Ames stood in the window nodding and handing out Royal Waves to those passers-by who noticed him and even some to those who did not. It was important for him to remain firmly in the public eye. Keeping a high profile with his readers was a necessary part of staying on top in the community of Gloucester and District.

He was, though, becoming a little concerned. He felt that his writer, Lomax, would not be able to produce top class copy indefinitely. If he could he would have still been employed by one of the nationals. Ames needed some extra insurance in order to keep the pressure on the Record. Something that would again arouse his reader's interests and keep most of the advertising revenue flowing into his company's bank account. Wynstanly must be struggling by now, possibly close to bankruptcy. One more push would send him and his second rate rag into oblivion. The boring fat fool with orange hair would be gone and the Clarion, his Clarion, would scoop all of the lucrative advertising business. Ames was comfortably well off. Even with a share of the advertising available in the county his paper always made a good profit. But Ames did not want a share he, like Wynstanly, wanted it all and, like Wynstanly, would go to any lengths to get it. Ames hated Wynstanly. Wynstanly hated Ames. On the surface the two men were polite and cordial to each other. Underneath, each would have no qualms about disembowelling the other with rusty fish knives.

Ames caught sight of Sophie just as she was passing on the opposite side of the road. He knew Sophie was a very good worker, very conscientious, very attractive. Someone who he would dearly like to have working for him. In fact working very close to him. The thought of Sophie working for him as his 'right hand' caused him to try and attract her attention. But she did not see his agitated gesticulation. She was pre-occupied with looking in her handbag. As she drew level with the Clarion's offices she pulled out a bunch of keys but failed to notice the slip of folded paper that came out with them and flutter to the pavement. Ames tapped on his window but, again, she did not notice and hurried on.

Vaughan Ames left his office and crossed the road to the spot where the note had landed. He glanced around, to see if Sophie was coming back, before picking it up. He unfolded the paper and read the hand written message it contained. His eyes widened and his mouth opened and shut like a gaping goldfish. He was, for a moment, rooted to the spot in amazement at the incredulous contents of this piece of paper that had escaped from the handbag of Wynstanly's most efficient employee.

He recovered his composure, slipped the note into his jacket pocket and quickly retreated to the confines and privacy of his office. Inside he sat at his desk took out the note and read it again – and again – and again. Three times he read the words that were undoubtedly written by Sophie's own hand. Three times they conveyed the same unbelievable message. He read it once more, this time aloud:

'MR. WYNSTANLY IS VERY HAPPY TODAY BECAUSE HE IS IN LOVE WITH MR. DOBSON.'

At first he could not believe his eyes. Now, on reading the note aloud, he could not believe his ears. But it must be true. Sophie, sensible, reliable Sophie would not make such a shocking statement without foundation. He put the note down on his desk, lent back in his chair and the smile on his face just grew and grew.

So it is true. Just as everyone thought. Wynstanly is a brown hatter – a limp wrist – a poofter. YES! YES! Now I've got him – got him by the balls – Oh no!, better leave that to Dobson – HA! HA! HA!

Ames then spent a good five minutes rocking with laughter, occasionally banging his desk with an accompanying 'YES' as the huge amount of damage that he could now inflict on his rival and arch enemy became more and more apparent. YES! Wynstanly's advertisers would desert him in their droves. YES! We will make a killing on revenue. YES! The Record will never recover and will eventually disappear up its own back page. YES! YES! HA! HA! HA!

When he finally calmed down, it occurred to him that closet gays sometimes became so starry eyed when in that they would throw caution to the wind and proclaim to the world their leanings, not to mention bendings, in a grand coming out ceremony. Ames also considered that, such was the numbness of twenty first century senses, the Gloucestershire public may not even raise an eyebrow at the announcement that Wynstanly was as bent as a fish hook and had been buggering at least one of his male employees for goodness knows how long.

He gave this some thought before penning a note of his own, this time for the attention of his editor:

Hold Monday's front page. The headline will be LOCAL NEWS PAPER PROPRIETOR IN GAY SEX ORGY. I will give you the full story before the weekend.

Ames had been in the business long enough to know that – 'it's not what you say it's the way that you say it – that's what gets results'.

9

"Hey! Have I got news for you Birdman?." Jack Prosser had only just got through the door of the Tip when Dobson called out to him. Jack looked up. Ned was smiling and leaning on the bar with the remains of a pint of bitter in one hand. Rosie was in the process of putting two more pints down in front of him.

Jack shook his head and smiled back as he ambled across the room. The previous evening his mate had been as miserable as sin with his face down to his knees and looking as though he had all the troubles of the world on his shoulders. Now, here he is as bright as a button and looking like he has just found a million pounds. He would never fathom Ned out as long as he lived.

"Evening Rosie."

"Good evening Jack." Rosie avoided Jack's eyes as she set about drying a pint mug that she had dried at least once before that evening. There was more than a hint of a blush on Rosie Diez's cheeks.

As a lover of the natural world Jack Prosser was used to reading its signs. It held few secrets from him. He had the key to most of Mother Nature's cupboards. In the human world, as far as reading signs and spotting what was going on around him was concerned, he was as blind as the bats hanging under the eaves of Jake Brown's hay barn. He would never in a hundred years have guessed that seconds before he walked in Ned had propositioned Rosie with some robust chatting up. Straight to the point, with no back passes, so that scoring some time after shut tap would be a mere formality for the Tip's bar room ram.

Ned drained his glass and picked up the two full ones.

"Over here pal." He nodded towards their table in the

corner, next to the fireplace. "Get this down your neck and I'll fill you in".

Jack had been looking forward to his early evening drink. There had been no photography work for the paper and he had spent a long hot day tending his garden. As he gulped down four large swallows of beer he could see Ned over the top of his glass grinning broadly. There were few dull moments when Dobson was around. Jack Prosser got the feeling that this was not going to be one of them. He put the half emptied glass down and wondered what Ned had up his sleeve. He was not prepared for what was coming.

"How do you fancy a trip to Copenhagen?"

"WHERE?"

"Copenhagen old butt. Capital city of Denmark. Land of long legged blond lovelies and 'probably the best lager in the world'," Ned said, giving a passable impression of a Gloucestershire Orson Wells but failed to impress the Birdman who had little theatrical knowledge.

"Can't say that I like lager much," Jack said impassively. "It gives me wind. Anyway I can't afford it. I'm only part time you know."

"It's free."

"What – the lager?"

"No dick-head. The whole lot. Air tickets, hotel room, meals and –." Ned reached inside his trouser pocket and pulled out a plastic card and proceeded to wave it under Prossers' nose. – "EXPENSES."

"What's that then?" Jack said eyeing the card suspiciously.

"This, lovely boy, pays for all the beer we can drink, all the food we can eat and all the women we can –."

"But what is it?" Jack interrupted.

"This, pal, is the Records Gold American Express card. Gilt edged, stone wall guaranteed and virtually bottomless."

"When did you pinch that then? I thought Denzil was skint."

"I didn't pinch it," Ned said, angry at Prossers under excitement. "Wynstanly gave it to me. Along with the authorisation to use it as many times as I liked."

"Drunk was he?"

"HE WAS AS SOBER AS A BLADE OF GRASS. God Prosser I sometimes wonder how you and me ever became mates. You can be as dull as ditch water when you want to be. WATCH MY LIPS. This Thursday morning you and me will be on a plane heading for Denmark and four days of the most fun you can have on someone else's money. GOT IT?"

"I suppose," Jack said. But he hadn't got it at all. Instead he settled for downing the rest of his beer and waiting for the full story to come out, which would not be until Ned had put his own glass down. In one go Dobson emptied it then let out a great belch of beer gas before continuing.

"Remember the European Cup Final in 1992?"

"Er! yes," Jack said, trying to rewind his memory back to the moment in question.

"When we were all here shouting for the Danish team to knock over Holland, who were the favourites."

"Oh! Yes!" Jack exclaimed brightly as he suddenly remembered the hot Saturday night in June when they were all glued to the television in the bar shouting for all they were worth.

"Well, Wynstanly wanted me to do a weekly piece on the Treaty of Maastricht. I ask you – have you ever heard anything so sucking as that? I mean to say who the bloody hell wants to plough through that load of old bollocks? It would be like trying to read treacle. Anyway, I couldn't be arsed with it all so this morning I hinted, just hinted mind you, that the Danes got the cup so long as their Government came back with a YES vote for Maastricht."

"And Wynstanly swallowed it?"

"Wynstanly would swallow seaside donkey shit if he thought he could crap it over Ames's head. He now thinks that we are on to the biggest story ever. One that will make him famous, earn the paper loads of cash for the exclusive rights and ultimately sink Vaughan Ames with all hands. So we, my dear old butt have been assigned to dig out the story."

"But there is no story. You made it up."

"Hey! steady on Prosser old pal. I didn't make it up, he did. All I did was throw him a few scraps. He was the one who turned it into a meat and two veg Sunday dinner."

"So what are we going to do about it then?"

"What we are going to do, my little bird lover, is to go to Copenhagen this Thursday and have the time of our lives. Then, we shall come back with a roll of film of some Danish politicians and tell Denzil that they threatened us with a libel writ if we so much as mention one word of such an outrageous lie."

"But I don't know any Danish politicians." Jack said with a frown. "I'm more into natural studies – foxes in Tewkesbury High Street – that sort of thing."

The Birdman was beginning to worry. He had always lacked Dobson's panache, not to say bottle, when it came to tampering with the truth.

"Prosser, old boot, do you think that Denzil knows any Danish Members of Parliament? He couldn't tell one from an ice cream seller. Come to think of it neither could I. Hey! look at this, two empty glasses and two men dying of thirst. It's your shout." Ned passed the glasses to the Birdman and nodded him towards the bar. "Hey! and no chatting Rosie up – she's already spoken for."

Indeed Rosie Diez's firm and desirable body had been booked by Dobson for a bout of carnal activity just as soon after shut tap as she could get away.

Rosie had caught the attention of the Tip's male patrons the day she came to be interviewed by Charlie for the vacant barmaid's job. So engrossed in their own male trivia gossiping were they that, at first, they failed to notice her arrival. However when she lent on the bar casually chatting to her potential employer the talk stopped abruptly. Wave after wave of lustful looks and lecherous longings hurtled towards her. Never had a forty year old female tail looked so inch perfect inside a tight pair of blue denims. A close fitting, white, cotton T-shirt was tucked into her jeans and stretched tightly over her shoulders and straight back. The top was cut low at the back and even lower in the front. In the mirror directly behind the landlord, the first person to notice the most perfect pair of breasts he had ever seen was Ned Dobson. As he had seen and fondled more than his fair share over the years, that made Rosie's breasts pretty special.

"Who the flop's that?" Dobson said in an audible whisper while the rest of his mates remained open mouthed and immobile. Charlie Harries had no hesitation in employing her. Not for his own sexual gratification of course. The rotund and jovial landlord's vices were confined to food and drink and plenty of them, but he had not failed to notice the effect she had on his hero Ned. So he regarded putting her on his payroll as more of an act of friendship than a duty to his business.

Rosie Diez had acquired her surname within weeks of deciding not to return to Bristol Airport at the end of her Club 18–30 holiday. Instead she stayed on in Magaluf and married Ramon Diez, a fiercely handsome and bronzed Spaniard who she stole from under the very noses of a clutch of local girls, much to their annoyance.

Rosie spent an idyllic ten years helping Ramon extract money from the would be wind surfers and para-gliders of the once yearly athletes.

Ramon scoffed at the futile attempts of those burnt shouldered, chicken legged, beer gutted air-heads out to prove their sporting prowess in front of an adoring throng of topless bimbos. He laughed at their attempts, but kept a very straight face when he took their holiday Pesetas off them.

Rosie slipped into the Spanish life with ease, enjoyed

the food but kept her desirable body in perfect shape. They were long, idyllic days and nights of sun, sand, sangria and sacks full of sex.

In time Ramon fell into the same trap as the brain-deads who turned up each year trying to impress the opposite sex. As he got older, so the impulse to roll back the years grew stronger. As he approached forty the urge to prove that he still had it in him ended his marriage. Rosie caught him screwing an eighteen year old from Rochdale who was stretched wide legged over a Black Cobra surf board.

For Rosie it was goodbye Spain hello Monks End and a job serving behind the bar of Charlie's pub. Charlie's decision to take her on proved a good one. Bar takings doubled when she was working and many a regular could be found drowning in her sparkling green eyes whilst offering to take her home and show her what a real man was made of.

Rosie wasn't fooled. She had been around. She could tell the difference between a talker and a doer. If she had taken up their offers of sex she knew that most of them would run, like frightened rabbits, back to their warrens to cuddle up to their old does shaking with fear at their lucky escape. Most of them, but not all. There was one she knew would not run away. Perhaps that was the reason he attracted her. He was not particularly good looking, not very tall, not in the greatest of shape but he was the only one in the bar who was sure to see the job through to its glorious climax. She also knew that it was likely that he would drop her for someone else before she could say same again. But he made her laugh and she fancied him like hell and when, just before Jack Prosser had walked in, he had asked if he could walk her home that evening she felt her legs turn to jelly. Something she had not experienced for a long time.

As Prosser stood waiting for Rosie to pull two more pints he again failed to notice the eye contact that she and Ned were making over his shoulder. Jack's head was full of doubts and confusion over this so called assignment that Dobson had got them both tangled up in.

He was a home bird. He never did like straying too far from the nest. Unlike Dobson who seemed to spend most of his spare time in someone else's. And what would his wife have to say about it, him spending nights away from home without her.

"I don't think Agnes will like it mind," he offered, turning around to face Ned.

"No problem Jacko old pal," Ned said with a wave of his arm. "Leave her to me. By the time I've finished telling her how famous you're going to be when your photographs get sent around the world she'll have your bags packed before you can spit."

"Oh! Righto then," Jack said and turned to pay for the beer. "Foreigners!"

"What's that Mr. Prosser?" Rosie asked.

"Foreigners Rosie. Denmark will be full of foreigners."

"And most of them Danish I shouldn't wonder Mr. Prosser. That'll be three forty-two please."

Foreigners – foreign food – foreign language – flying Thursday – FLYING THURSDAY? Jack Prosser's knees suddenly went wobbly. He had only flown once in his life. Last year Agnes' nephew had paid for them to go and see them in Canada and the flight back was rougher than any theme parks wildest nightmare ride. When he stepped off the plane at Gatwick he vowed that he would never get on another one – ever. He had spent a lifetime watching buzzards soaring on the thermals, hawks swooping on their prey, swallows and swifts darting about high in the sky but the thought of once again being up there with them made his head spin and his pulse quicken. Flying was strictly for the birds, definitely not for him. Dobson had gone too far this time. He was more than happy with his quota of photographing carnivals, fetes and country shows. Political intrigue was not his cup of tea at all. Especially political intrigue that had been invented by Ned and involved both of them leaving the ground far below. This he was not looking forward to as he returned to his seat with the two pints of bitter.

"Good crack eh?" Ned said. "Four days of drinking and debauchery and all paid for. Cheers Denzil." And he raised his glass in salute to their unwitting benefactor. Prosser looked glumly into his beer.

"Cheer up you miserable sod. We'll have a great time. Wynstanly can't complain. It's not my fault if he let his imagination run away with him. Anyway he owes us. Look at all the work you have done for him and what has he paid you? Peanuts pal that's what. If you were working on a proper paper, you'd be on ten times as much. Besides it's not coming out of his pocket is it. Just a couple of bob that the tax man won't get his hands on eh?"

The Birdman did not understand the workings of credit cards. He had never got involved in that sort of thing. He did understand though, that if the card Denzil had handed over gave Ned access to cash, then it would be more than just a couple of bob that the tax man was not going to get his hands on.

"Er! – We couldn't go by boat could we?" he asked hopefully.

"Boat? International journo's don't go by boat. They'd never get their stories. You wouldn't catch Kate Adie heading for the world's hot spots on the boat. It would be all over by the time she got there. We're going to be part of the jet set brigade Birdman old boot. So fasten your safety belt and prepare for take off."

Jack sank deeper into his seat and resigned himself to the fact that Thursday would probably be his last day on earth. He would be reported missing presumed drowned in an air disaster over the North Sea. He fastened his fist around his glass and took a long pull. His pulse rate was rising again. He finished his drink and looked at his watch.

"Ten to seven, time we were off home." He said.

"You can. I'm staying." Ned replied.

"But your food – your meal – it will be on the table in ten minutes."

"And it can stay there."

"But – Gwendolyn – won't she be –?"

"Couldn't care less if she is or not. She can stick her Chicken Fricassee back up the chicken's arse as far as I'm concerned. I'm here for a session matey, a real good session," and he glanced across at Rosie.

"Oh! All right then," Jack said with a shrug of his shoulders. If his mate insisted in staying then that was up to him. "See you tomorrow then."

"See you tomorrow Jacko."

It was nearly midnight by the time they had walked back to Rosie's flat. It had been a very encouraging walk for Ned with his arm around her slim waist and no adverse reaction from her when he occasionally let his hand drop down on to her bottom. At the flat Rosie laid some cushions on the floor and Ned set about the job in hand.

Some girls Dobson just had sex with – a quick bonk in the Tip's car park. Others, the special ones, he made love to. He could, at the right time with the right girl, be a very attentive lover. For twenty minutes he went through his well tried and tested routine. He had probed her mouth with his tongue before gently kissing her on the neck, on her shoulders and on the tops of her breasts. While his mouth was doing its work he slowly ran his hand over her tummy and down the inside of her thigh. He repeated these actions again and again and Rosie for her part responded with some sensuous touches of her own. He did all this and more but for the first time in his life it was not working. Nothing – zippo – zilch – no reaction whatsoever.

It wasn't Rosie who did not want to come out to play it was Ned's willy and he just could not understand why. After twenty minutes of fruitless effort he rolled onto his back and sighed.

"Sorry Rosie. I'm gutted. I can't believe this."

Rosie lent over and kissed him on the forehead.

"Too much beer maybe? You sank a few tonight. Maybe you should have given me a bit more thought," she teased.

"No! No! I've never had brewers droop before," Ned said sitting up. "I'll bet you it was that cow that done this to me."

"Which cow was that?" Rosie asked.

"That cow Gwendo. When she stuck her foot in my bollocks. She's done for me. I'll never be able to do it again."

Thirty minutes later a dejected Ned was kicking his shoes off at the bottom of the stairs of his own house. He could see through bleary eyes that his pyjamas had been thrown, no hurled, down the stairs. Indicating that his presence was not welcome in the nuptial bed and that he would, not for the first time, have to sleep in the spare room. He slowly climbed the stairs, undressed, slipped into the single bed and instantly fell asleep. Totally oblivious to the fact that the Chicken Fricassee he was lying on was still quite warm.

10

The seething mass of sweating, heaving bodies flayed about under a myriad flashing, rotating coloured lights. The tightly packed heave filled to overflowing that which was known as the dance floor. What that coagulation of youthful humanity were doing could never in the most imaginative of minds be called dance. In the true sense of the word, dance should have purpose and pattern. There may well have been an underlying and unspoken purpose in the heaves gyrations that evening but pattern was most definitely out of the window.

A rain dance had pattern. This was no dance designed to induce precipitation. A fertility dance had pattern. Ah! then you may say, what they are doing is a First World, 21st century equivalent of a tribal fertility dance. If that were so then ask yourself this question – 'who, among the female of the species on this hot and steamy night, would want such a dance of fertility to prove successful when later she lays spread-eagled and panting across the bonnet of her mates xr3i?'

More likely would not the opposite be true? That this dance be a dance of infertility. Invented by the female and designed to vigorously shake the male scrotum to the point where his sperm would not know whether it was coming or going. The antics of the Greater Acned Night Clubber is, without doubt, a great, great imponderable and worthy of debate among the most highest of the lands Thinkers. If such a debate were ever to take place, they who thought would do well to consider the incidental music that accompanies this dance. And being brains of the highest order they would no doubt arrive at the conclusion that for such a cacophony of noise to be classed as music must be regarded as more accidental than incidental.

All this of course mattered not one dribble to those boys and girls who were sublimely ecstatic in this dome of pleasure known as The Blue Lagoon Club. And it mattered even less to Frankie Ferranti as he stood looking out through his two way mirror at this Tuesday night's intake. Ferranti's jittery and nervous disposition when in the company of Chief Inspector Touber the previous evening had now gone. It had been replaced, with the help of a dash of the company's excellent products, by the smooth calculating and confident manner for which The Voice had employed him.

He stood and watched the crowd for a moment. What they did, how they did it, why they were doing it and who they were doing it to was of little interest to him. His only thoughts were for the wads of money his business would extract from their young pockets before they vanished into the night exhausted and convinced that they had had a great time.

Tuesday night at the Lagoon was ladies night. A night when the fair and gentler sex were allowed in free of charge. And in order to guarantee that they turned up in eager and anticipatory numbers, the cabaret for the night was THE FIVE BIG BOYS. A quintet of throbbing masculinity who strutted their hunky funky stuff about the stage. Tearing at the velcroed seams of their uniforms until their glistening bodies were exposed to the point where those young girls who had led sheltered lives fell down on the floor in a faint.

You would not need to be a great philosopher to reason that with such a hoard of young, female bait wriggling and writhing in his net, Frankie Ferranti could be certain of shoal upon shoal of marauding males surging through the doors of his club. Lustily oblivious to the inflated admission charge and the equally overpriced fashionable lager available at the bar and which tasted little better than Mexican buro piss.

How eternally grateful he was that the common senses of the rampant male were invariably dulled by the probability of a quick shag.

As Frankie Ferranti stood watching this multitude of bouncing breasts and thrusting crutches one of his minions extracted himself from the centre of the mob and made his way through the tables. The man was one of the clubs mixers. Employed specifically to mingle with the clubbers in order to pick up gossip, stories, scandal, information, anything which could be stored for possible use some time in the future. His mixers also kept him informed on who was dealing and what they were dealing in. Frankie tolerated a few of these small time sellers who used his club as a market place. Tolerated them because if ever there was a raid on the club by drugs squad officers, they would be the ones who would be picked up. And as they were not connected with Frankie then no connection could possibly be made by the visiting officers. Frankie would look suitably shocked at such a thing going on in his respectable establishment and offer as much assistance as he could to have them locked up for a very long time. He also tolerated them because he had them continually in his sights. Captured on the clubs closed circuit television with a dossier on each of them waiting for a time when he would need a favour. They were not taking much business away from him. The stuff that he dealt in was destined for a much higher class of user. It amused him greatly when he would read of the street value of a confiscated haul. The real value of such a confiscation was not down on the street but up in the apartments and playgrounds of Aristo's, Rock Stars, Leaders of Countries and Captains of Industries. Here was where the big money was made not on the street or on the floor of a sweaty little disco in Gloucestershire.

The mixer was now passing a message, mouth to ear, to a broad shouldered heavy. When he had delivered the message he began to point someone out in the midst of the crowd. Frankie followed the line of the mans arm but he was unable to pick out the person they were looking at. His men had been given instructions to bring back news of any clubber who intended to travel this weekend. To complete the task that his own employer had set him he had reasoned that it should be relatively simple to pursuade someone, packed and with passport at the ready, to taste the sensual delights of Copenhagen as a prelude to their two weeks somewhere on the Costa.

He would offer them first class air travel, five star hotel accommodation and a guarantee that they would be back in time for their Airtours package to the sun. All for the simple task of exchanging bags with an old family friend who would meet them in Copenhagen's Tivoli Gardens.

This, Frankie had decided, was preferable to putting the screws on one of the small time dealers in the club, if only for the fact that they may already be known to the police. Frankie's Heavy was now outside and knocking on his door.

"Come in."

"Mr. Ferranti, there is a girl in tonight who has spoken of making arrangements for two people she works with to travel to Copenhagen this Thursday."

Call it luck, call it coincidence, call it whatever you will. In any event Frankie Ferranti took a moment to absorb this amazing and fortunate news whilst, at the same time, concealing his own amazement with all the skill of an accomplished poker player.

"Do we know anything of her work colleagues?"

"She works at the Record – the weekly newspaper."

This time a shiver ran through his whole body and visibly stiffened his shoulders. The memories of the previous evenings game of golf with the Record's Managing Director Denzil Wynstanly, Vaughan Ames and Chief Inspector Touber flooded into his mind.

Luck? Coincidence? Fate? Frankie now had a nagging doubt. These connections were too close for comfort. If anything should go wrong – any mishap. The chain he was dangling from had links in it that were too close to home. If he had a choice he would sever the connections now and walk away. But he had little choice, no choice in fact. The Voice wanted – insisted – on a result. An away win, nothing less, so –.

"Bring the lady to my table and send over a bottle of the House Champagne, unopened, along with a bottle of my reserve Bollinger ready to pour and two glasses."

At work Sophie Davies was efficient and hard working. She enjoyed her work and demanded and got reasonable amounts of respect from her drooling and pathetically lecherous male colleagues. At night she partied, drank Buds and brandies and let her long blond hair down with a vengeance. This night she was taken by surprise when one of the clubs bouncers tapped her on the shoulder and invited her to join Mr. Ferranti at his table.

"ME?"

"Yes miss. Follow me please."

She followed the man from the dance floor, giggling self consciously at the chorus of whistles and "oo's" from her friends. When pretty girls were invited to join Mr. Ferranti it was assumed that talk of the weather or unemployment figures would not be on the agenda. Frankie watched her. He noted that in spite of the obvious fact that she had been drinking she had gathered her composure and was now walking towards him with the kind of elegance that cat walk models spent hours perfecting. Already he was admiring her tall slender form, her long tresses of blond hair and pale, flawless complexion. He rose to greet his guest and, as she came nearer, realised that she was even more stunning than his first thoughts had conveyed.

She wore a pale blue, silk mini-dress held up by two thin shoulder straps. Every move she made caused the dress to shimmer and flounce and attract attention. She could have graced any of the worlds glittering night spots. What was such a creature doing here in what was little more than a gaudy shack in the country?

"Mr. Ferranti – this is Miss Davies from the Record."

Frankie took her hand, bowed gallantly and gently placed a kiss on the backs of her fingers. Everything about her was simply exquisite. He guided her to her chair and not until she was seated and comfortable did he take his own place at the table.

"Miss Davies you must be wondering why I have asked you to join me. Do not be alarmed, there is no sinister or ulterior motive behind the invitation. It is simply that each night I indulge myself by surveying the many charming ladies who come to enjoy themselves at my club. I look out for one who is worthy of receiving a prize. Sometimes there is a winner sometimes there is not. You are by far the most glamorous lady ever to have entered my most humble establishment. Please accept this bottle of our most expensive champagne as a small and meagre reward for gracing our club this evening."

Frankie stood up to hand Sophie the bottle of house champagne which she accepted with an "Oh!" and a giggle of surprise. She held the bottle on her lap and cradled it in her arms like a doll.

"I try to make these presentations as discreetly as I can. A public presentation with all its incumbent jeering and shouting would debase such a charming moment don't you think? Now please join me for a little celebration of our own to mark the occasion."

Frankie became aware that he was oozing great ladles full of his Italian charm this evening. He had never felt the urge to turn it on so much. He was more than a little smitten by Wynstanly's girl. He poured two glasses of his favourite Bollinger and handed one to Sophie who had now given up on composure and was beginning to enjoy the attention. Touching his glass with hers he stared deeply into her dark blue eyes.

Whole armies of randy leering males stimulate their under-used genitalia by sneaking sly and contemptible looks up young girls skirts. This Latin lover would not dream of indulging in such an ignoble and sordid act. If those depraved and dishonourable wretches could see what he could see, simply by looking into the eyes of a sensuous woman, they would instantly go blind in a deluge of sexual excitement.

"To a very, very beautiful lady." The words were announced slowly and deliberately and he did not fail to notice the dilation of Sophie's pupils as he spoke them.

Sophie crossed her long shapely legs and tried to stifle a shiver of excitement of her own by taking two large mouthfuls of the best champagne she had ever tasted. Frankie instantly topped her glass up. In spite of his earlier denial she could tell she was being seduced by this charming, good looking, rich Italian. She could find no reason to offer any resistance. Besides, back on the dance floor her friends were all being moved on by slobbering blobs of sweating puke who's most imaginative pulling lines were little more than 'show us your tits darling'. Seduction by this beautiful, charming, intelligent male body sat opposite her was infinitely more desirable. She again half emptied her glass and again it was instantly refilled.

For his part Frankie was beginning to feel a chemistry between them which, if fused and joined together could easily move the earth to the point where the Cotswold hills would find themselves sinking into the Bristol Channel.

It was the voice of The Voice from within that reminded him on this occasion there was a piece of important business that must come before such temptingly delicious pleasure.

"So, we are honoured to have a member of the famous Record here tonight. I was with Mr. Wynstanly just last evening. He seemed to be in very good spirit. Things are going well at the newspaper? He is getting over his problems with Mr. Ames at last?"

"Oh! yes – yes thank you. Things are going quite well at the paper." Sophie answered, unsure as to the meanings behind the questions.

There was little that went on in the county that Frankie Ferranti was not aware of. His team of information gatherers did not confine themselves to listening to the night club chatter. They were equally observant during the daylight hours. Even so it was common knowledge that the two papers were each fighting for pole position. To her credit Sophie Davies had never let anyone outside work get the impression that her boss's paper the Record was desperately struggling to survive. If all Mr. Frankie Ferranti wanted this evening was confirmation that the Record was on the verge of collapse then he would not get that information from her. She watched him pour more champagne into her empty glass. Had she drank that much already? On the other hand if her reticence brought to an end the charming attention she was receiving well –.

In the event Frankie's next sentence changed the subject and kept her loyalty intact.

"Of course, the Record only deals in local news – no foreign assignments for your journalists I would imagine."

"Well, as a matter of fact Mr. Ferranti –"

Frankie cut her off. "Call me Francesco," he said, leaning towards her and filling her glass yet again. "It is a name that only my closest friends use. So you Sophie, you must call me Francesco. It will please me greatly."

This was the final sign for Sophie Davies. This incredibly sexy man was out to pull her and she now had no intention of putting up any sort of fight which may cause him to lose interest. She was getting a taste for Bollinger. It was complimenting the brandies and Buds and all three were doing something rather splendid to her ovaries. She drained her glass for what was the fourth? fifth time? who's counting anyway? and watched him slowly, with the artistry of an accomplished pourer of fine wines, refill it.

So, she thought, if calling him Francesco pleased him then the item she now had on top of her list of things she would like to do to him would send him into heavenly orbit.

"Well Francesco," she said, also leaning forward, unaware that with her right hand she had begun to caress the neck of the champagne bottle she was holding in her lap. "Mr. Dobson and Mr. Prosser are about to go to Copenhagen – this Thursday in fact. I booked the flights myself but I haven't yet been told why they are going." Sophie giggled at her original thoughts on this unusual foreign excursion.

Dobson was known to the night club owner but Prosser was a name that meant nothing to him.

"So, the notorious Ned Dobson is on the trail of an international scoop maybe. No wonder there is secrecy. It does not do to let your rivals know what you are up to. And even if you Sophie did know the purpose of their visit I am sure that you would not turn out to be a kiss and tell person." KISS was delivered with deliberate emphasis.

Sophie countered with the most alluring look she could muster. "Oh! no Francesco. I wouldn't dream of KISSing and telling."

Frankie was very impressed. She was now trading innuendo with him. The fact that she had already consumed two thirds of a bottle of his best Bollinger may have helped but it also showed that the girl had spirit. He liked a girl with spirit and imagination. He particularly liked that touch with the neck of the champagne bottle. A relationship with this girl had great and long lasting possibilities. Maybe a trip to Florence to look for a wife would not be necessary after all. But, business first.

"And Mr. Prosser, he is a reporter also?"

"Oh no! Mr. Prosser is our photographer." Sophie laughed at the thought of dear, old Jack Prosser being a hard nosed reporter. It just could not be.

"Ah!" Frankie said, "a reporter and a photographer. What a perfect combination don't you think so Sophie? Like elegant wine and expensive chocolate. A perfect combination. Just perfect."

To compare Ned and Jack with elegant wine and expensive chocolate was an analogy out of touch with reality. A comparison more closer to ground level would have been far more appropriate. But then what would an educated and sophisticated Italian gentleman know of beer and pork scratchings? Sophie forgave Francesco instantly as she gazed into his eyes and hiccuped. Her self control and last remnants of composure were slipping away.

Francesco was on top and thrusting home his advantage. She thought that somebody should investigate the aphrodisiac properties of Bollinger champagne because she was beginning to get the kind of ache that she only reserved for special boyfriends.

"And all their travel arrangements have been left in your very capable and sensitive hands." He reached over the table, removed the champagne bottle from her lap and placed it on the floor. Taking hold of her hands he began to caress them gently with his thumbs. Sophie started to shake.

A voice inside her head was screaming 'say something say something but make it intelligent'.

"Yes – Yes – they're booked on the first flight out of Heathrow and will be staying at the Plaza hotel – the agent suggested it – I hope it will be all right."

"The Plaza Hotel!" Frankie's delight was obvious. "I know it well. It is in fact just across the road from the famous Tivoli Gardens and opposite the railway station. They will be most comfortable there. Most comfortable. Be assured my beautiful Sophie that your arrangements are perfect, absolutely perfect. But then from perfection we must only expect perfection must we not?"

He bent his head forward and kissed her on both of her hands. He then pulled her across the table so that she was out of her chair and her face was almost touching his. He placed three more soft kisses, one on each of her flushed cheeks and the final one on her trembling lips. It was total meltdown.

"I would now ask you to do me a small favour."

"Yes! yes!" she thought, "anything anytime – now in fact – let's do it now – here over the table – under the table – on the bar – anywhere just let's do it" she was pushing her mouth on to his trying to get her tongue down to his tonsils but he was – PULLING AWAY?

"Sophie! – Sophie, tomorrow it is my birthday," he said, gently fending her off. "I thought that I would have to celebrate alone. You must do me the honour of joining me. My driver and I will pick you up at seven. I must leave you now. I must work this evening. Ciau my dear Sophie. Ciau, until tomorrow." Frankie stood up kissed her once more on the top of her head and walked away leaving her draped across the table.

11

In the breakfast room of St. Tyllow's Vicarage the Reverend Rhys Howells was coughing, spluttering and dangerously close to a terminal fit of choking. Mrs. Mumford, his faithful and attentive housekeeper, was vigorously patting his back in an attempt to dislodge whatever was apparently blocking his windpipe. The robust, some would say fat, housekeeper, was a determined woman. Determined enough to ensure that her much revered and holy employer would not choke to death whilst in her care, even if it meant dislodging a vertebrae or two. The primary cause of her beloved, Welsh Reverend's near apoplexy came not from the contents of the cereal dish which lay on the table in front of him but from the contents of a letter which lay by its side. The simple acts of reading its startling contents and swallowing a mouthful of Cornflakes at one and the same time had proved too much for his brain and windpipe to cope with in unison. The rotund and normally genial Mrs. Mumford was unaware of this and continued to beat the crap out of her vicar's shoulder blades.

Howells, at last, managed to hold up a hand as a sign that he was capable of taking control of his breathing without any outside assistance. He had been unable to convey this message to her by word of mouth for as fast as he took in a much needed breath the energetic Mrs. M. was beating it back out again. Eventually she called it a day.

"There, there sir. Is that better? Bones in the milk I shouldn't wonder. Here, let me get you a glass of water."

"No – no Mrs. Mumford," Howells gasped. "It's quite all right thank you very much. You've done more than enough for me already. I'm very grateful. Now if you would be kind enough to let me get on with finishing my breakfast."

"Then let me take all this away from you until you get your breath back and feel well enough to deal with it."

The attentive and doting housekeeper moved to pick up the letter in question along with the rest of the morning's mail. But, even whilst recovering from the misfortune of a mouthful of cornflakes attempting to gate-crash the airspace of his lungs, Howell's reactions were a mite quicker than hers and he grabbed the pile away before she could get her chubby little hand around it.

"No, that won't be necessary Mrs. Mumford," he said, waving the bundle of letters at her. "There is work to be done here you know. God's work that must not be held up for the want of a little breath. If you would be good enough to get on with your own work then I shall get on with His."

The starry eyed housekeeper dutifully departed the breakfast room full to the very brim with admiration and love, albeit unrequited, for the great and good reverend Rhys Howells. When she had closed the door and the sound of her footsteps had faded away down the passage Howells read the letter again. This time more slowly and with a little more ecclesiastical foresight than at the first reading.

The letter was written on the headed note paper of the Fors-Bowers Estate, Wiltshire. Here the formality ended for the body of the letter was not typed but hand-written and in a hand that was strong and bold and belied the near ninety years of the writer. It read:

'Howells, what the devil are you playing at? That fool Dobson has written to say that you will vouch for Those Two Women. What's all this Howells? If you have told him about William and you think you can get your hands on my money then you have got another think coming. Get Dobson off my back or I shall blow your cosy cleric's life sky high, you miserable little hypocrite. R.F.B.'

The second reading of Randolph Fors-Bowers letter to the Reverend Rhys Howells did nothing to lighten its original impact. On the contrary, reading it for the second time not only sent his senses reeling yet again but threw up a host of questions. HOW did Mr. Dobson know Randolph? WHERE was the connection? WHY was it necessary for Mr. Dobson to write to Randolph and tell him that his wife and Mother-in-Law, who he (the vicar) had yet to meet, were regular churchgoers and that he (the vicar) would bear witness to it? WHY did Randolph refer to Mr. Dobson's wife and mother in law as "those two women" and in such a hard-nosed way? Where were the connections? Did Mr. Dobson's wife and Mother-in-Law have connections with Randolph?

A few days earlier Ned had followed up his own letter to the vicar with a visit to the vicarage. After which, the Reverend Howells was left in no doubt at what was required of him. In the unlikely event of anyone asking he should confirm the regular attendance of the Dobson family at his church. The whitest of white lies, to be told in return for a financial remuneration. A simple enough task. Helping a parishioner out of a domestic jam was almost an act of charity.

But, the 'unlikely event' had just been upgraded to a 'definitely happened'. And, the 'anyone asking' has emerged as the terrifying Randolph Fors-Bowers.

Rhys Howells searched his memory for clues to the answers. He cast his mind back to his meeting with Randolph just a month ago. It was the first time the pair had had come face to face for almost fifty years. He had gone back to Wiltshire to complete the confession that he had tried to blurt out on that March evening some forty-four years ago. The evening when he stood, army padre's cap in hand, outside the front door of the Fors-Bowers stately home ready to make a clean breast of things. Ready to confront Randolph and tell him that he would marry his daughter Gwendolyn who, in one unguarded moment that New Years Eve he had made pregnant.

He remembered standing there filled with remorse and shame and on the verge of pressing the doorbell when it occurred to him that he had been a victim of circumstances. It was, after all, a New Years Eve party given by Randolph himself. Celebrations were in full swing. Everybody was relaxed, happy and drunk. He was no different from anyone else. He had feelings and expectations just as much as they did and he joined in with a vengeance.

Passions were high and so were, on the night in question, Gwendolyn's skirts. He had been overcome by an unstoppable urge of sexual longing and gave her one. Who could blame him? She was an attractive young woman. The first one he had come in close physical contact with for years. The forbidden fruit was ripe and there for the taking.

Who could blame him? He questioned again and in a flash he had removed his finger from the door bell, replaced his cap, did a sharp about turn and marched out of the Fors-Bowers lives for ever – or so he thought.

The burden of guilt that Rhys Howells had carried for years finally ground him down and sent him on a journey of pilgrimage back to the scene of his original sin. He continued to remind himself of his meeting with Randolph in the hope that a clue to a connection with Mr. Dobson would somehow emerge, but there was nothing. It was, after all some years ago. Was it '91 or '92? He couldn't remember. He did remember though that Randolph had been nothing less than indifferent when this clerical stranger had turned up on his doorstep admitting to being the father of one of his grandchildren. The old man's 'couldn't care less' attitude threw Howells into a quandary. He had arrived fully expecting to receive a good horsewhipping or, at the very least, a tongue lashing from an angry and irate old man. But not a bit of it, not a hint of anger, not a crumb, not a morsel, nothing. Fors-Bowers senior showed not the slightest interest in Howell's unbosoming of latent guilt. The only thing that Howells had learnt was that Gwendolyn had called the child Magenta.

But Howells desperately wanted, achingly needed to make reparation for his unholy misdeed. If only for the fact that the first of his sexual encounters with a member of the opposite sex had so whetted his appetite that it had sent him spiralling off into a dual lifetime of preaching and perversion. Try as he might, since that first penis insertion he had been totally unable to stop himself from screwing around. There had never been any shortage of amorous lady parishioners who regularly turned up on his doorstep in need of counselling and guidance.

His most pleasurable moments however came from his trips to the centres of Gloucester and Cheltenham. Here the, seemingly, clerically correct vicar had become a well-known and accepted figure amongst the rough and tumble regulars of the back street bars. They had taken to him as one of their own as he flitted from pub to pub spreading the word to the assorted congregation of the straight and the bent. An assorted congregation who were never likely to turn up on his doorstep.

Safely cloaked in anonymity he moved amongst the villains, the pimps and the prostitutes. Accepting as many double Jim Beam's as were offered and never refusing donations for his church restoration fund. By the end of his rounds he had consumed a heart warming quantity of JB's and pocketed more than the required 20 pounds for his final act of the evening. Thirty, trembling, minutes in a darkened shop doorway with his favourite Gloucester dame de la nuit Tania, also known as Magenta.

But not my dear reader to the vicar. Not for now and, possibly, not ever. That piece of, very useful information shall be our little secret. One day we may let the clerical cat out of the bag. Allowing it to chase the rat of St. Tyllow's in and out of the church pews. But, until that spiteful day ...

Whether it was her black lycra top, which she filled so magnificently, or her red leather mini skirt which she protruded from so magnificently, or the fishnet stockings and suspenders which were – just magnificent. Whether it was one or all of those magnificent three that caused his blood to surge to an appendage not normally visible from the pulpit he was not sure. There was, however, something about her that made him feel quite at home. If for one millionth of a micro second Rhys Howells had realised that one of 'those two women' was his illegitimate daughter with whom he was unwittingly having an incestuous, not to mention pricey liaison, then he would have been on the first train out of Gloucester Central before his Bishop could say, 'Bless you my son'.

For this life of lechery and debauchery the fallen vicar increasingly felt the need for reparation. His first act of atonement was a face to face with Randolph and a willingness to do penance and take his punishment like a man. The penance that Randolph eventually handed him seemed, at the time, to be all too trivial. Hardly matching the dual sins of shagging and impregnating Randolph's only daughter Gwendolyn. Howell's penance was to travel to London and make contact with Randolph's son William, a junior under secretary at the British Foreign Office.

William would never have risen to such a position without the monetary aid and influential guidance of his powerful father. Left to his own devices William Fors-Bowers would have amounted to nothing. He would have spent a lifetime stumbling around in his father's footsteps until he finally inherited the estate and would have, without a shadow of a doubt in Randolph's mind, eventually lost it to some foreign speculator. Randolph was pleased that William was at the foreign office. His position had proved to be most valuable. His son never failed to keep him informed as to what people were up to – particularly foreigners. Randolph had an aversion to foreigners.

* * *

Howell's once crispy cornflakes had now relaxed into a soggy, orange mess. He stared into the bowl and tried to make some sense of his meeting with Randolph's son, William. He replayed the day's events over and over in his mind searching for a connection that would explain this letter from Randolph.

He had travelled to London by train, taken a coach to St. Katherine's Dock. He found the small patisserie near the entrance, seated himself at a table next to the window and placed the black attaché case, that Randolph had given him, onto the floor and by his feet as instructed.

A moment later William Fors-Bowers arrived. Howells knew instantly that it was him. If William had not been blessed with his father's strong character then, at least, he had his distinguished looks. He remembered that William, smartly dressed in a three-piece pin-stripe and carrying a case similar to that which the vicar had brought, greeted him like an old friend.

"Nice to see you again. Have you ordered?"

"Er! no – not yet."

"Allow me then."

William placed his case by the side of Howells' and ordered a pot of tea and two buttered scones. For the next few minutes they had proceeded to exchange meaningless pleasantries about the weather, the opulent yachts moored in the dock and the superb quality of the buttered scones. When the scones had been devoured Randolph's son had made his goodbyes and left. He took with him the case Howells had brought and left the one that he had arrived with. Nothing more than that. An exchange of cases mixed with a sprinkling of inane conversation. No clue there as to why Randolph had written to him so brusquely.

Perhaps from his conversation with the other one? A tall, good looking, blond gentleman wearing a loose fitting, beige suit who spoke with a foreign accent – possibly Scandinavian – and who had greeted him in a similar way to William but this time ordered coffee and

Danish pastries. He, also, had a case. Exactly like the one that Randolphs' son had just left behind. He, also, placed it next to the vicar.

The following minutes mirrored the preceding ones to the point where the foreigner left with the case that William had left leaving behind the one that he himself had come in with. Perfectly straightforward, except that the bag that William Fors-Bowers had brought with him contained a bankers draught made out to cash for two million pounds and twenty thousand Danish Krone. The bag which the Scandinavian gentleman had left and which Howells had to take back to Randolph contained nothing more than a note written in Swedish. When Randolph eventually got it translated it made him very cross indeed.

In replaying these events not one single clue had been revealed to Rhys Howell's memory as to how Randolph Fors-Bowers came to know about his association with Mr. Dobson.

Howells, again, stared vacantly into his pulpy breakfast cereal. He pushed the bowl away from him, reached into his cassock and pulled out a silver hip flask. Flipping over the hinged top with his thumb he raised the flask to his lips and took a long pull on its rejuvenating contents.

He was mid way through a third slug when the door of the breakfast room was flung open revealing a forceful Ned Dobson wrestling with a determined Mrs. Mumford who was doing her best to block his effort to gain entry. For the second time that morning Rhys Howells found himself coughing and spluttering. This time it was a fine spray of single malt whisky not semi-skimed milk that descended on to the breakfast table. While he coughed and spluttered Ned and Mrs Mumford continued their own struggle.

"The vicar is very busy – you should not go in – he is not expecting you ..."

"Leave off woman! – the vicar and me are old friends – 'course he'll see me."

Ned turned the defending housekeeper around and directed her back up the passage with a sound slap on her generous backside.

"Oh! Oh! you disgusting little man – I've never been so – Oh!"

As the flustered housekeeper scurried up the passage Ned back-heeled the kitchen door and walked over to the spluttering vicar.

"Having it on our cornflakes now are we vicar? Can't fault you pal. Went down the wrong way though by the seem of it. A good slap on the back will sort it."

Howells tried to wave Ned away but he was unable to prevent a second backslapping. Dobson, however, was not as persistent as Mrs. Mumford and after two hefty whacks between Howell's shoulder blades sat down at the table and eyed up the silver flask.

"Any chance of a –?" Ned nodded in its direction.

Howells, now in a trembling and nervous state, nodded back and Ned polished off a days ration in one single swallow.

"The thing is vicar I'm off to Copenhagen in the morning. A bit of newspaper business." Ned touched his nose and winked as though the vicar was in on the scurrilous scam that he was about to work on Denzil Wynstanly. "And I was wondering whether you had heard anything?. That is, has anybody been asking about the wife and her mother?"

Howell's mouth open but no word would come out. He wanted to ask Mr. Dobson how he, his wife and Mother-in-Law were connected with Randolph Fors-Bowers but the events of morning appeared to have damaged his vocal chords.

"Only, you know what to say if anybody should ask don't you? They're regular churchgoers – W.I. – WRVS. – pillars of society and all that stuff. I'll see you all right vicar. Trust me – I'm a journalist." Ned held up the silver hip flask. "Oh! And they are off this stuff mind – they haven't touched a drop in years don't forget. Mind you, fat chance of Gwendolyn ever giving it up, the drunken old cow."

Rhys Howells froze. The whisky induced colour drained from his cheeks. His quivering face now whiter than his own dog collar.

"Gwe – Gwe – Gwendolyn?" Howells stammered.

"Yes! Gwendolyn, the wife's mother. Permanently pissed she is. Anyway, must be off, got to get packed and sorted. See you when I get back." Ned took another pull at the silver flask, placed it on the table and left. "Cheers."

The Reverend Howells sat staring at the kitchen door that Dobson had just slammed behind him.

"Oh my God!" He muttered. "Oh my good God! Gwendolyn is his Mother-in-Law – Oh my God! – Magenta is his wife! Oh My God!"

He left the kitchen and stumbled down the passage to his study. Kneeling down, in front a cupboard, he unlocked the door and took out a large brown bottle marked Holy Water. He topped up his depleted silver hip flask with some of its amber coloured contents, replaced the bottle and locked the door. As he was stepping out of the front door of the vicarage he turned towards the passage and, in as strong a voice as he could muster, called out. "I'm going out Mrs. Mumford. I shall be out all day and most of the n – don't wait up."

The Reverend Howells hurried off in the direction of one of his "other" parishes. There, the obliging Tania would smother him with comfort and succour in this, his hour of desperate need. He was away from the presbytery, still totally unaware that he was heading for yet another, costly incestuous assignation.

12

The Scandinavian Air Services flight SK.500 pulled away from Heathrow's Terminal 3 at precisely 7.25 am. As the D.C.9 taxied to its take off position Jack Prosser's eyes were glued to the attractive air stewardess who was miming the safety instructions to a voice coming from the aircraft's public address system. The female announcer spoke perfect English but with a Scandinavian accent that had a cadence and rhythm not unlike a Gloucestershire farmers way of singing the spoken word. This similarity was lost on Prosser, as was the attractiveness of the mimer. He was more concerned with trying to memorise the locations of the exits, the life jackets, the oxygen lines, the sick bags, the life jackets the exits, the sick bags, the exits, the oxygen lines, the exits – the exits – NO PARACHUTE?? He came within an ace of putting his hand up to ask the question.

If he had taken his eyes off the object of his undivided attention for just one minute he would have noticed that he was the only one paying any sort of attention to her. A quick glance around the cabin of the aircraft may have reassured him that there was absolutely nothing to be worried about. His fellow passengers, mainly business people and probably seasoned air travellers, were apparently relaxed and reading an assortment of morning papers, magazines and books. Air travel was after all, safer than negotiating the M5 – or so Ned had assured him.

If an honest and truthful poll had been taken from his fellow travellers, Birdman Jack Prosser would have learnt that the majority of them were just as apprehensive as he was – with the exception of Ned. His only concern was whether the beer in Denmark would come anywhere near as good as a pint of Charlie's best. The rest of the passengers were aware that take off was the most dangerous moment of flight. If the aircraft, upon reaching its optimum speed, stubbornly refused to part company with the runway their final destination would be closer to Trafalgar Square than Copenhagen Airport. The arm waving antics of the smiling air stewardess would then count for nought.

"We're up Jacko!"

"What?"

"We're up mate. Look at the ground, miles down it is."

Prosser declined the offer. Apart from the fact that he had absolutely no intention of looking anywhere except straight ahead, he and Dobson were separated by another passenger. A tall, good looking, blonde haired gentleman dressed in a loose fitting beige coloured suit.

Ned's ticket had given him a window seat and Jack had a seat next to the aisle. The man who sat between them, and who spoke with a Scandinavian accent, had obligingly offered to change places with either one of them in order that they may sit together. Ned had refused to budge and Jack wanted a free run to an exit should the need arise.

Travel changes people. Once free from the boundaries and force fields of their natural habitat behaviour patterns change considerably. The sober become drunk, the meek turn uncharacteristically aggressive and the reticent start talking. Jack Prosser started talking to the man in the beige suit. Not just returning polite conversation but taking the lead and forcing the issues. On discovering that the man was a Danish businessman en route back to his capital city Jack proceeded to expand and expound, not on his beloved ornithology, but on the Treaty of Maastricht. A subject about which not even Ned, the Record's so called Political Commentator, could utter more than a sentence or two before resorting to flannel.

"You see," Jack said, "the Treaty of Maastricht

marks an historic moment. A new stage in the progress of European integration. It deepens the solidarity between the people of the European continent while at the same time respecting their own history, culture and traditions."

The beige suit nodded in thoughtful agreement. The Danes after all were well versed in the finer points of this famous document. Their Government had, in the short space of a few months, held no less than two referendums on it. Two referendums on that dogs breakfast of illogical cobblers was more than enough for any electorate – one more and Amnesty International would have waded in. Whilst Prosser continued his oration Ned surveyed his early morning in flight meal of cold chicken, cheese, celery and black grapes. Not even Gwendolyn would consider serving up such a meal at eight o'clock in the morning. Strange eating habits these foreigners have got, he thought. Not to worry, when in Rome. He set about clearing his plate whilst at the same time cocking a quizzical ear in Prosser's direction and wondering whether altitude had affected his mate's brain.

"You've got to hand it to the European politicians," Prosser continued, "they are determined to promote economic and social progress within the context of the accomplishment of the internal market."

"Mmm, Ya! Ya!"

"They have got to create a closer union among the people of Europe. Where decisions can be taken in accordance with the principle of subsidiarity."

"Ya! Ya! Subsidiarity."

"Subsidiarity my balls." Dobson said, unable to keep his nose out of the conversation. "what does subsidiarity mean anyhow? No one knows pal – no one."

The Dane in the beige suit received a prod in his thigh and a spit of chicken and cheese roll as Dobson proceeded to emphasise his point. "I'll tell you about this Great European Union pal. We would be better of out of it. THEY don't like us and we don't like THEM.

Always has been and always will be pal, you mark my words. Federal Government? Single currency? Who wants it, eh? Not the rank and file pal, I'll bet a Euro to a plate of fish and chips – not the rank and file. It's the politicians pal, they're the ones who can see what a nice little earner it is. One huge gravy train which they're all busting their balls to get first class seats on and will do anything to keep it chugging along the track to their own El Dorado . Even fiddle the votes on the Maastricht referendum, like your lot did."

It was an unfortunate moment for Ned to deliver his libellous and dangerous piece of hearsay as the Dane was in the act of swallowing a mouthful of coffee. The remark agitated him so much that he spluttered large blobs of the liquid on to the crotch and inside leg of his immaculate beige suit.

By the time flight SK500 had touched down at Copenhagen Airport the Dane had received chapter and verse from a well informed Jack Prosser along with considerably less informed interruptions from Ned Dobson, including Ned's own libellous opinion that the Danish football team would not have won the European Football Cup unless their Government could guarantee that the country would vote in favour of the Maastricht Treaty.

"You gave that guy a right old pasting," Ned said as they walked along the airport concourse. "Where did you learn all that stuff on Maastricht? I thought you and politics didn't mix"

"Well, I thought I'd better find out something about it. So I borrowed that copy you keep in your shed. We are on an assignment you know. We ought to bring some sort of story back for Wynstanly – he is paying for it after all."

"So he is, so he is. Let's have a pint to celebrate his benevolence."

"It's only just gone half past nine." Jack said looking at his watch.

"No it's not. They're an hour up front over here.

Look at that clock, it's way past ten thirty. Charlie will be opening the Tip any minute now. Come on we'll have one before we pick our bags up."

Jack decided not to bother to question Ned's logic and a few moments later was pulling hard on a glass of the smoothest lager he had ever tasted in his life.

In one of the airports toilets a tall blond man in a stained beige suit was bending backwards like an arthritic limbo dancer thrusting his damp crotch at the surge of hot air coming from the hand drier on the wall. One hand clung to the drier to prevent him falling over the other held a mobile phone to his ear.

"Someone has talked Lars. Your man in London, William, he is from the county of Wiltshire isn't he? I have had the passenger list checked by our man at the airport. These two are from Gloucestershire, the bordering county. There must be a connection. I believe one of them may be a reporter, the tall grey haired one. The other one, the short stubby one, with glasses, must be a photographer. Get Jan outside the airport quickly and have them followed. Make sure Jan never lets the tall one out of his sight, he is the clever one."

13

Wonderful, wonderful Copenhagen. Capital of one of the world's oldest Kingdoms. Kobenhavn, the merchant's harbour. Absalon's city. Founded by the Bishop Absalon in 1170 A.D., on the island of Slotsholmen, a piece of land almost at the heart of the present capital. With the harbour to its south and canals on its North, East and West sides. On this tiny island the good Bishop built his bastion to hold back invaders.

Whilst his fellow countrymen, those heathen hordes of the Great Danish Army, ravaged and plundered Northumbria causing the monks of Lindisfarne to flee for their lives, and in some cases their virginity, Bishop Absalon was laying the foundations of what was to become a most welcoming and friendly city.

Compare a tough and uncompromising Geordie with today's laid back fun loving Copenhagener and you would have to wonder where such Danish aggression came from. The more intuitive among you may conclude that it had been left fertilising the loins of those who had been ravaged and plundered.

On the ruins of Absalon's castle there now stands Christainborg, home of the Danish Parliament and its 176 members. The Copenhagen that Ned and Jack Prosser had descended on is a city of distinguished charm and elegance. Ancient and post war architecture flanks its abnormally wide main streets.

Dobson and Prosser were now in the enviable position of being able to take in the incredible views of the city from the famous Round Tower, or visit the Rosenborg Palace, or stroll through Deer Park or Frederiksberg Castle Gardens. Maybe browse among the variety of shops and stores in Stroget, the Walking Street. A pedestrian shopping area that stretches from

Town Hall Square by the side of Hans Christian Anderson Boulevard through five streets as far as Kongens Nytorv, The Kings New Square.

Here in the city's largest square, they would find The Royal Theatre and Opera House. The magnificent and luxurious Hotel D'Angleterre under the watchful eye of a bronze statue of Christian V, astride a trusty steed. In Stroget they could purchase anything from tourists souvenirs to expensive pieces of Royal Copenhagen porcelain or a Bing and Grondahl hand painted figurine. A pause outside the window of Halberstadt's, the jewellers and goldsmiths, may reward them with a glimpse of the Golden Train on one of its runs through this exclusive store. The train and wagons made of 18 carat gold. The engine encrusted with almost two hundred diamonds. Each of its four wagons carrying a cargo of rubies, sapphires, emeralds and still more diamonds. If it is true that diamonds are a girl's best friend then Halberstadt's Golden Train must be her eternal soul mate.

When they had wearied of window-shopping, the two men could relax in any one of Stroget's numerous bars, restaurants or pavement cafes. Or, indeed, in any one of Copenhagen's two thousand, multinational eating places. The finest French, Italian or Spanish cuisine was there for the eating. High class Indian, Chinese, and Mexican restaurants all available for the discerning gourmet.

The Danes have a word in their language called Hygge. It is a passionate word. Not for pillaging, raping and plundering, or splitting an enemy from head to toe with one mighty downward stroke of an iron sword. No, Hygge refers to the Danes passion for enjoying themselves at every opportunity. The visitor to Copenhagen will soon be engulfed by Hygge and will quickly succumb to the Danish way of enjoying all manner of pleasures in a most relaxed and unselfconscious way.

On the other side of the coin the Nation that spawned those early heathen Viking rapists and pillagers, also appears to have seen the religious light. The Danish Capital has dozens of places of worship. Buddhism, Baptist, Lutheran, Catholic, Methodist or Muslim, whatever your particular ecclesiastical leaning, ask and you shall receive.

The betting odds on Dobson and Jack Prosser attending any one of Copenhagen's houses of assorted Gods were so long as to be virtually incalculable. The odds on them ignoring the many splendours and enchantments of this beautiful city and opting for the splendours and enchantments of the female performers of Copenhagen's night clubs were not even on offer.

Jack Prosser stood at the window of his room at the Plaza Hotel. When he had eventually mastered the computerised key and entered the room allotted to him he had been amazed at its size and poshness. Wall to wall carpet, not a piece of lino' in sight. Bedspreads that matched the curtains. Two large dark oak wardrobes, a highly polished mahogany writing desk and an identical cupboard which, when he opened its doors, revealed enough drink and snacks to kick start a medium sized wedding reception. Colour television, telephone by the side of the bed, classy pictures on the walls. It was a palace compared to the homely standards of his and Agnes' cottage back home in Monks End.

Few if any of the Plaza's guests would be aware that they were staying in an hotel that had been built by Royal Command. Given the simplicity of Jack Prosser's life and his limited knowledge of the world beyond the boundaries of his village life you, my dear reader, can safely assume that Jack would be one of the many who knew nothing of the hotel's history.

When construction of Copenhagen's Central railway station began in 1906 King Frederik the Eighth ordered that an hotel be built close by. In the 1920's and 30's it was patronised by Barons, Counts, Landowners and very, very rich people. On each floor was a small mailbox which was connected to a larger, brass, mailbox in the lobby. This main mailbox was emptied each day, thirty minutes before the post train was due to leave. The hotel had its own tailor who would sit in the traditional cross-legged position while he repaired the guests clothes, particularly those who had been granted an audience with the King.

After dining in the hotels restaurant guests would take coffee in the elegant Tapestry Hall where they would be entertained by a famous pianist. In 1970 the Tapestry Hall was renovated and renamed The Library Bar which Forbes Magazine selected as one of the world's five best bars. A fitting place for two of the world's biggest drinkers to drink in.

All this enlightening and historical information had never been available to Birdman Jack Prosser. Even if it had he would have given very little consideration to it. Jack Prosser had something else on his mind at that moment. He stood at the window, looked out across Bernstorffsgade and down into the Tivoli Gardens. He was oblivious to the fact that he was looking at one of the most famous pleasure gardens in the world. The majestic concert hall, open air theatre, fun fair rides, lakes, fountains, trees, buildings all meant nothing to him. The only thing that did register in Jack's anxious mind were the numbers of people milling about.

Already, at mid-day, the Gardens were filling up with people, lots of people.

Jack turned and walked over to the bed were he had placed his case. He unzipped it and took out the blue and white flight bag that lay on top of his clothes. He frowned and shook his head. How did she talk him into it?

"Please Jack," she begged, "the Tivoli Gardens are just across the road from where you are staying. All you have to do is take the bag to the bandstand and hand it over. The man will give another one to bring back. Keep it to yourself. Don't tell a living soul, especially not Ned. Please Jack, do it and I'll love you forever."

She had cupped his face in her hands and kissed him on the side of the mouth. Sophie Davies could be very persuasive.

As he held the bag in his hands he wondered if he could even find the bandstand, never mind the man wearing a light grey coloured suit and a black shirt with some words written on the front. Words which he had already forgotten, and which Sophie wouldn't allow him to write down.

His worries were interrupted by the ringing telephone. He ignored it. It must be a wrong number. He didn't know anybody in Copenhagen. The ringing stopped, but only for a moment. When it restarted Jack slowly picked up the receiver.

"Hello –"

"Jacko you old bugger. Where have you been? I've been ringing for ages. On the bog were you?"

"Who's that?"

"It's me you pillock. Who do you think it is – Eric the Viking?"

"Ned? – Where are you? How do you know this number?"

"I'm in my room – God Prosser you've led a sheltered life pal. Listen! Swill your face and meet me down in the bar in twenty minutes. Bring your camera. You can bag a couple of shots of the Parliament building then we can wine women and song it for the rest of the weekend. Put your skates on, I'm as dry as a crisp."

Jack Prosser put the phone down and wandered over to the window for another look at the Gardens. Again he shook his head. How did he let himself get talked into coming to this place, this Danish place. One day he would stand his ground and say NO. One day. But today he was thousands of miles from his own garden and Agnes his wife. She'll be knitting him another cardigan for Christmas while he is out of the way. Less than half a day out from Monks End and Jack Prosser was already missing his home. Homesick and annoyed with himself that he had allowed Sophie to sweet talk him into this bag swapping arrangement. He didn't get on easily with strangers. Foreigners were an additional complication and the more he looked the more

109

crowded Tivoli was getting.

Jack Prosser was a worried and worrying man.

On the pavement opposite a man was casually strolling along the side of the Tivoli boundary wall. He was wearing a light grey Borden Anderson tailored suit with a pale blue shirt and a neatly tied brown and cream patterned tie. He had been casually strolling up and down the pavement for half an hour or more. He now stopped and looked up to the third floor of the Plaza Hotel. At one of the windows he could just make out the figure of a tall grey haired man looking out. The casual stroller jabbed at the numbers on his mobile phone and made his report.

14

Reports and messages in and out of the Danish Capital were markedly up for an average Thursday lunch time. Randolph held one in his hand marked "PRIORITY – ACTION IMMEDIATE". It had just been passed to him by his son and heir William who, even though he was sixty two years old still, whimperingly, turned to Father in times of trouble.

"What are we going to do about it?" William asked when he handed Randolph the memo. "I mean to say – who are these two? – How did they find out?" He was now pacing up and down the drawing room carpet nibbling the end of his thumb. "They didn't hear it from me. I've said nothing – nothing to anyone. Besides, I don't know anybody tall, grey haired, weather beaten – or that other one – short and stumpy with a moustache, and needing a haircut. Who the devil are they Father?"

Who the devil were they indeed? The tall grey haired one rang no bells in Randolph's memory but the description of the second nosy parker had set off a whole clatter of alarms. While William continued to pace the carpet Randolph considered this latest unwanted predicament. If Dobson and the vicar were in league and after his money, and the fool reporter was now sniffing around in Copenhagen then a very hairy situation was brewing. Unless he acted sharply the amount of manure hitting the fan would make his heavy duty muck spreader look like a Christmas toy.

"If this gets out –," William's voice began to shake. "I'm only three years away from my pension – index linked – I'll be blackballed at the club – a laughing stock. I wish I'd never got involved. It wasn't my idea in the first place. You –" A cold stare from Randolph pulled William up in his tracks.

The House of Commons headed note paper in Randolph's hand had been delivered to William's Foreign Office cubby-hole by messenger. The personal runner of a Member of Parliament well known for his anti-Maastricht views and his downright fire spitting aggression against the whole idea of the European Community. The Member in question was rumoured to be high up in the Dangerous Little Army. A hard core band of Euro sceptics, who had been hell bent on blocking every Governmental move towards ratification of the Treaty of Maastricht. It was also rumoured that Old money was helping to bolster the cause.

Randolph finally screwed up the paper and tossed it into the log basket by the side of the large fireplace which was patiently waiting the arrival of winter. William decided that winter was too far away for the destruction of such incriminating information. Taking a match from a large box permanently on the mantle piece he set fire to it and dropped it into the empty hearth. Randolph, also, had decided on action.

"Tell Jenkins to bring the car round. I'm going to church," he snapped.

"Church? – Church father? – We are chapel – Isn't church a little on the high side? Lighting candles won't do us much good."

* * *

The 1950's, grey and black, Austin Princess slowly rounded the corner at the top of Church Street, Little Hardwicke and glided to a halt outside the door of St. Tyllow's vicarage. On the back seat a tweed suited Randolph sat legs apart with both hands resting on a silver topped walking cane. He was staring down at his highly polished brown leather boots as though waiting for them to offer advice on this unexpected dilemma he now found himself in.

The boots were old friends, studded at the toe and heel. The sound of him crunching along the lanes and paths of his estate encouraged his already toiling workers to an even greater frenzy of activity. The steel studded footwear had also toe-ended more than one band of travellers who had thought that they would be safe for the night in some far flung corner of his land.

They could still play a major part in solving his present predicament. A swift stab in the area of the parsons nose may be enough to scare the pants off the vicar, allowing Randolph to get the cleric to do exactly as he was told. Randolph was a man of instant reactions. Jump in feet and brown boots first. The questions may be asked at some later date. However, the long and thoughtful journey to Little Hardwicke had thrown up a couple of points not entirely in favour of such domineering action.

A vicar frightened pant-less just may do a bare-arsed runner into oblivion. On the other hand he may just as easily run to the nearest solicitor for a bean spilling session that would delight any lawyer eager for a sniff of lucrative litigation. It was not every day that clients brought tales of international scandal and intrigue. Tales of a respected Wiltshire landowner's futile attempt to bribe International football teams into capitulation in order to keep Britain British.

"Minimum wages?" Randolph was often heard questioning. "Shorter working weeks? Paid overtime? – Damn fools are trying to ruin us – never did trust the French, or the Germans."

The thought of the repugnant Dobson rooting around Copenhagen, possibly on the verge of discovering that he, Randolph, and a number of other prominent and wealthy anti-Europeans had each lost a small fortune trying and failing to change the course of history was another reason to consider treading very carefully whilst walking over the Reverend Rhys Howells. Being taken to the cleaners by Scandinavian crooks was one thing. Being held to ransom by a third rate newspaper reporter who was married to his grand-daughter was another. He would also have to call in a favour or two from sources high up the Governmental ladder if this problem was to be sown well and truly watertight. Leaving it all in the dithering hands of a vicar whose alcoholic and sexual fetishes made the Canterbury Tales read like a collection of fairy stories would not do at all.

Mrs. Mumford showed Randolph into the vicarage study.

"I'll tell the vicar that you have arrived sir."

Rhys Howells had heard the boots in the passage and was right behind her.

"That's quite all right Mrs. Mumford. I am aware of Mr. Fors-Bower's arrival." Howells said and he eased passed her into the room. As he passed her his upper arm brushed the outer extremities of Mumford's ample bosom. Moments of actual physical contact between housekeeper and the object of her unrequited love were rare indeed. A gentle biceps to bosom brush did not rank anywhere near a full frontal fondle but it was close enough to send her nipples pointing skywards. She suddenly felt an urge to leap upon him. Press herself all over him, into his shoulders, his chest, his face – "OH!" – but she could not. They had a visitor.

"If you would be kind enough to bring a pot of tea and a few digestive biscuits Mrs. Mumford. I am sure our visitor would be grateful for some refreshment after his long journey." He ushered his flushed and throbbing housekeeper away closing the door behind her.

The Reverand Howells was remarkably self assured and calm this warm July day, considering that he was again in the presence of the man who's daughter he had romped with so passionately and indeed so effectively all those years ago. He hiccuped.

"Oh! Pardon me." He reached deep down into his cassock pocket, pulled out a packet of mints and popped one into his mouth before offering one to Randolph.

"Lunch was a little heavy today. I find these are a perfect antidote to Mrs. Mumford's cooking."

Randolph declined the offer. Ignoring the whiff of

alcohol he sat himself down on the leather sofa near the window, legs apart and hands resting on top of his walking cane. The vicar remained standing for a moment his left hand in his cassock pocket twiddling his extra strong.

Why, thought Howells, do old men, very old men that is, always sit with their legs apart. And women, particularly fat old women, they do the same. He had watched them in the church hall. Clusters of fat elderly ladies nattering, legs wide open, airing their differences. He had witnessed sights on parish evenings that were almost enough to put him off his lustful visits to the public houses, but only almost. Randolph's voice brought him out of his daydream.

"Well er – vicar." Already Randolph was struggling. Polite conversation did not come easy. "How is Dobson?"

Even in his relaxed state Howells was still sharp enough to appreciate that wealthy, powerful, Randolph Fors-Bowers had not travelled over from his Wiltshire country seat just to inquire after the health and general well-being of a reporter on the local paper. Even if the reporter was the husband of the illegitimate child of the landowner's daughter. And even if he, Howells, was the father of the illegitimate child of the landowner's daughter who the reporter was now married to. The trite enquiry as to the said reporter's health and general well-being was too incongruous for words.

Howell's appreciation of the moment, and subsequent reminder of the worrying facts surrounding the question, drained the single malt stimulated colour from his cheeks for the second time in as many days. His left hand released its grip on his mints and proceeded to gently caress the other occupant of his cassock pocket, a silver hip flask.

"Er! – Mr. Dobson? I believe that he is in Copenhagen at the moment. Some newspaper work no doubt."

Randolph tapped his cane on the floor. So it's true. The fool is on to it. Damn newspapers – if he finds out –

he must be stopped – he MUST be stopped.

Randolph tapped his cane once more.

"Copenhagen? You say. Pity – pity." Randolph shook his head and frowned a false frown.

"A problem Mr. Fors-Bowers?" Howells asked, curiously.

"A problem indeed vicar." Randolph was now head bowed and suddenly cloaked in the mantle of one who's very life blood was draining away. "Old age vicar, old age. Time to right a few wrongs – before it's too late." He said, raising his head. "Check the fors and against – see if the ups and downs balance out."

Howells wondered which particular 'up and down' Randolph had in mind.

"We all make mistakes vicar. None of us are perfect. We are all at the mercy of life's temptations EVERY minute of the day." The silver topped walking cane was banged down on the floor in emphasis. Randolph's Chapel upbringing was beginning to show and the Reverend Howells found himself caught in the stare of a man who was delivering a message but not with the words that he was actually speaking.

"I need to see Dobson – talk to him – I – I've been too hard on him – I can see that now. You will understand vicar. You must have people confessing to you every day I'm sure. Making their peace before the final day of reckoning. I realise now that life is too short for holding grudges."

The Reverend Rhys Howells was quite taken aback with Randolph's sudden humility and supplication. He felt obliged, as vicars do, to offer some words of hope and assistance. "I'm sure he'll be back soon. If he is on a newspaper story he will have to have – what do they call it? – 'his copy' ready in time for next weeks edition. Shall I tell him to contact you? Give you a ring next week perhaps?"

"That's very kind of you Reverend," Randolph said slowly, "but next week ..." Randolph paused. "Well, next week may be too late."

Never were words spoken with such conviction and truth. But the truth and conviction that Howells thought he heard did not match the truth in the elderly landowners own thoughts.

What? Some terminal illness – Randolph Fors-Bowers is finally at the terminus of life's bus route? Howells was stumped as his own thoughts criss-crossed his mind.

"I need to see Dobson now – today. It's vital. Time is running out."

Randolph was sounding more and more like a man within hours of coming face to face with the greatest landowner of all.

"Well I er! – I mean – he's in Copenhagen. He couldn't possibly get back today I'm sure."

"Tomorrow then. You must go and fetch him. It is urgent. Will you do that for me or, if not for me then for – for Magenta?"

Rhys Howells would not have given a second thought to scouring the Danish capital for Dobson even if Randolph was slipping into his final death throws before his very eyes. It would be nothing short of ludicrous for him to drop everything and set off on what could easily turn out to be a wild goose chase. However, the mentioning of Magenta caused him to reconsider. This trip to Copenhagen could be the beginning of a long journey down the penitent road to ultimate forgiveness.

"You won't be out of pocket of course."

The wad of money that Randolph was now waving in his hand clinched it. It looked to be made up entirely of fifties. Ten, maybe twenty of them it was difficult for Howells's eyes to get a precise number, nevertheless they were a great help in making up his mind.

* * *

Just a couple of dozen paces from the Record's front door is a row of telephone kiosks. As he approached them Vaughan Ames heard the phone ringing in one of the kiosks. He glanced across in time to see Frankie Ferranti enter the booth and quickly pick up the receiver. Ames slowed down in the hope of catching any snippet of conversation that he could turn into a newsworthy scandal but Ferranti appeared only to be on the receiving end of the conversation. Ames stopped to check his reflection in a shop cafe window before continuing towards the Record's offices.

* * *

"Frankie! Frankie! My dear Frankie. I hear we have a man at this very moment positioned in Copenhagen and primed to put right the failures of our late dear departed employee. I can but admire your organisational skills and commend your resourcefulness at moving so quickly, my sweet Italian pomegranate."

Frankie Ferranti frowned. What was the point of these calls. The Voice already knew everything. The man must have more informers than CNN. The point of the call was about to be made.

"I fear that I must now test your resourcefulness just a tincture further my honeydew melon. Tonight's arranged meeting at the Tivoli Gardens has been cancelled and will now take place on Saturday evening." Frankie's frown deepened. "My client, as you are aware dear boy, is a much travelling man and has had to fly to Brussels – such are the trials of being a great and important figure. The demands on him are excruciating. I know that by Saturday he will be waiting ablaze with eager anticipation for a quick and satisfactory conclusion to our little bit of business. But I am sure that the man you have chosen will not let us down. Am I not brimming with confidence that the man chosen by the, enchantingly, dependable Frankie Ferranti will complete the task in hand with aplomb and effortless magnanimity."

Frankie sighed – but only inwardly. The Voice must not have any indication that the chosen one, now in

Copenhagen and on the verge of doing the deal that very evening, was the best he could get his hands on in the time given. Especially as he had now discovered that Jack Prosser, although a dependable sort when it came to taking snapshots of carnival queens and councillors, was a simple soul. One who's rustic dependability would, most likely, turn to dust if he discovered that he was about to exchange one S.A.S. flight bag containing a kilo of high grade Colombian marching powder for a similar bag brim full of pounds sterling.

"Frankie, my extra virgin olive oil, I can't wait for our meeting this Monday, each hour, each minute, even the very seconds themselves cannot pass quickly enough dear boy. Until we meet my dear Frankie – Ciau Frankie CIAU."

Ferranti replaced the receiver and stood pondering this latest development. He reached inside his jacket and consulted a list of International telephone numbers.

"I'm sorry but Mr. Prosser is out at the moment. Can I take a message for him when he returns?"

The Plaza receptionist spoke perfect English and, no doubt one or two other European languages had Frankie taken the trouble to enquire. But he was in no mood to applaud the multi linguistic qualities of Danish Hotel receptionists. He replaced the receiver for the second time and checked his watch. He could just make the late afternoon flight to Copenhagen. An hour and a half flying time, a fifteen minute taxi journey and a little luck he could get to the Plaza before Prosser leaves for the bag exchange.

* * *

Vaughan Ames was now standing in the Record's reception area. Sophie had quickly appeared in response to his pressing the bell on the desk. His thoughts dallied briefly on that glorious day, hopefully in the not too distant future, when he would steal Wynstanly's best working girl away from under his nose. But until then –

the pupils in Ames's eyes visibly dilated as he took in the vision of sexual excellence flouncing and bouncing towards him in a skirt so short that it barely covered her exquisite bottom. And a top, a sleeveless, neck-less loose fitting top, beneath which there was no obvious signs of any bra-like garment. In the mid-day heat, even wearing his expensive and lightweight suit, Ames could feel a hint of moisture on his forehead. He took out his silk handkerchief and sent a cluster of small change coins scattering about the floor.

"Oh dear! We are throwing our money around today aren't we?" Sophie said. And, ever willing to please, the Record's pride and licentious joy bent down to gather the coins, leaning and stretching this way and that.

"The Clarion is doing extremely well at the moment," Ames replied as he, ungentlemanly, ogled her desirable form twisting and turning at his feet. "I like to think that all my staff have money to throw around if they wish. People who come to work for me do not find me ungenerous when it comes to being paid what they are worth."

It was a thin joke and a feeble attempt at a lure. Ames could have and should have done much better. Sophie handed Ames his money.

"Mr. Wynstanly is not in at the moment," she offered, parrying any further attack on her loyalty.

"Ah!" Ames gave a knowing and sage like nod of his head. "He's probably out on the golf course getting some much needed practice for the club final this weekend I suspect."

"NO," Sophie replied defiantly, even though that was precisely where Denzil was at that very moment. "As a matter of fact," and she will never understand why she said it but say it she did, "he's gone to Copenhagen with Mr. Dobson. They left this morning and we're not expecting them back in the office until Monday."

The brain is a powerful and complex organ. Scientific man may construct computers the size of the Himalayas. But a computer of any magnitude will never hold majesty over the brain of even the most dimmest of the planet's dimwits. The brain has the power to make the person within whose cranium it resides believe anything it wants that person to believe.

Within minutes of leaving the Record's office, Vaughan Ames had arrived at two conclusions. Wystanly and Dobson were most definitely having an unnatural affair and they had set off to consummate their union with a dirty weekend in one of Europe's most sexually liberated cities. Even, and the possibility was not beyond the bounds of probability, a gay marriage. The wedding snaps being taken on the steps of Copenhagen's Town Hall. They would not be the first, it HAD been done before.

As a newsman he had a duty to his readers to travel that very afternoon to the Danish Capital, track them down and procure photographic and recorded evidence of their vile and unnatural actions. If he moved quickly the story would be ready in time for next week's scandalous edition. The other conclusion had been finalised in his mind even before he had left the Record's reception area. As Sophie had bent down to retrieve his spilt cash she had accidentally proved the fact that her bra had indeed been abandoned for the day. In doing so she had exposed two of the most delightful breasts that Ames had ever set his admiring eyes upon.

He was now certain. When Wynstanly was disgraced and out of business Sophie would work for him. He just HAD to have those breasts on his payroll.

15

The Reverend Rhys Howells stowed his blue and white Scandinavian Air Systems flight bag into the compartment above his seat. It was a gift from the Travel Agent. Randolph had personally escorted him to purchase the air ticket to Copenhagen. The booking clerk had offered the bag as a token of the Airlines gratitude for flying S.A.S. Both of them, in fluster of checking flight times, had missed the clerks remark that S.A.S. flights to Copenhagen must be very popular as this was the third free flight bag she had handed out that afternoon.

Howells had done little travelling since leaving the army. There were the occasional sorties to neighbouring Cheltenham for some extracurricular spreading of the word but these were journeys of less than thirty minutes and did not require a travel case of any description. The flight bag would be more than adequate for his short stay requirements in the Danish Capital.

As soon as he located Dobson, appraised him of Randolph's change of heart and urgent need to make amends, he was sure that the man would have no hesitation in returning with him on the very next available plane. The cleric settled down in his seat, fastened his safety belt and prepared himself for take off. In a window seat three rows in front of the Reverend Howells, Vaughan Ames suddenly made a grab for one of the in flight magazines. Holding it close to his face he appeared to be reading it with a great intensity. This was not, though, the action of a short sighted and nervous air passenger. Ames was a seasoned traveller. But his seasoning had not prepared him for the sight of Frankie Ferranti coming down the aisle of the plane. Ferranti passed him by and took up his position at the rear of the plane. Ames slowly lowered the magazine and sat wondering what coincidence had put the Italian on the same plane as he, and heading for the same destination?

At the Police Headquarters in Gloucester Chief Inspector Touber was giving his counterpart in Copenhagen the description of a suspected drug dealer. One who had suddenly left the country and was now on a plane heading for the Danish Capital. Frankie Ferranti's card was well and truly marked.

16

It was just after five o'clock when Ned and Jack Prosser strolled back into the foyer of the Plaza hotel. After a couple of hours drinking in the hotels Library Bar, at significant expense to Denzil's credit card, they had spent the afternoon in the square outside the parliament buildings. Jack photographing and Ned chatting to anyone who looked remotely political in the square outside the Parliament buildings. It was a pointless exercise of course, but Ned had felt obliged to carry it through if only to placate the worried rumblings of Prosser. Jack had still not grasped the fact that they were on an all expenses paid break courtesy of Denzil and not actually chasing an international scoop.

Ned had also felt obliged, once conversation had been engaged with an unsuspecting Copenhagener, to raise the subjects of the vote on the Maastricht Treaty and the Danish football team winning the European Cup. But not both in the same sentence for fear of getting punched on the nose. The Danes for sure are a very friendly and obliging people but they may not have taken too kindly to the implication. Besides Ned had with him a tape recorder and a notebook. Some devious editing would produce the answers that Denzil wanted to hear.

The weather in Copenhagen was every bit as warm and sunny as it was in the U.K. In between photographing and recording, the pair had adjourned to a pavement bistro for, numerous and large, glasses of cooling premium larger. They failed to notice the Brodene Anderson suited gentleman who, since they had landed at Copenhagen airport, been following their every move. Even attempting to match them glass for glass, both in the Plaza's Library bar and later at the bistro.

By the time Dobson and Prosser decided to call it a day the suit was more pissed than he had ever been in his life at four thirty on a Thursday afternoon. He just about managed to phone his report in before the effects of the afternoon sun and the Premium Carlsberg took over, leaving him slumped and motionless across the café table.

Ned and Jack Prosser were now relaxing on one of the leather settees in the hotel foyer.

"Right! That's it for Denzil I reckon," Ned said. "We've got enough stuff to keep him happy. Now we can start enjoying ourselves."

"What do you think Denzil will do with it when he gets it?" Jacko asked.

"Run the story of course. It's cost him enough," Ned said as he patted the large wad of Danish kroner bulging in his back pocket which he had drawn on Denzils American Express card earlier.

"But it isn't true. You made it up."

"So who's going to know? Who's going to read the Gloucestershire Record in Denmark eh? Hardly any bugger reads it in Gloucester. It will be just another boring political story which no-one will take any notice of but will keep Denzil off my back for a month or two. Can't fault it I reckon. Now for God's sake Jacko stop worrying and loosen up a bit. It'll be time to get back on the plane before we can spit."

Their prodigious consumption of strong lager had indeed loosened the Birdman's inhibitions but Ned's mention of getting on planes instantly dissipated the afterglow. He sank gloomily back into the leather settee and took scant regard to Ned's sudden enthusiasm on noticing two pillars in the foyer covered in brass nameplates. Each of the brass plates named a VIP guest who had stayed at the Plaza. Dobson bypassed those from the stage of world politics and went straight to those from the stage.

"Hey? Look at this Jacko. Shirley Bassey, Tom Jones, The Bay City Rollers. It's a who's who of the entertainment world," Ned exclaimed. "Look here. Duke Ellington, Quincy Jones, Count Basie, Abba – you name them – they've all stayed here pal."

Ned was now stood up and checking out the names of the rich and famous who had graced the Plaza's accommodation.

"Hey! Just think Birdman you could be sleeping in the same bed as that blond out of Abba – what's her name? – Annie something."

Birdman Jack Prosser had no idea what her name was or even who Ned was talking about. He did, however, know that in less than two hours he had to find a perfect stranger, somewhere inside Tivoli, to swap bags with. Sharing a bed with a blond Swedish pop singer was more in tune with Ned's thoughts than his.

Even if Jack had known that the meeting was not two hours away but two days away and a Mr Frankie Ferranti was winging his way to Copenhagen to relieve the jittery Birdman from his unwanted duty, even with these facts and the large quantity of premium lager still coursing through his veins from the afternoon session Jack Prosser would never consider bedding a blonde Swedish pop singer or any other member of the opposite sex for that matter. He never wanted to come to Copenhagen in the first place. Ned had talked him into it. His wife Agnes would understand that. And he certainly didn't want to go out looking for a complete stranger in the amusement park of a foreign country. Something that Sophie had talked him into – Agnes would not understand that. On top of his anxiety he was now experiencing for the first time in his married life, guilt. He had been coerced, swayed and seduced by a sweet talking very attractive young woman.

The phrase 'no fool like an old fool' had been haunting him ever since they had left Monks End.

The two men returned to their rooms. Ned to consider the evenings entertainment and Jack Prosser to spend a fitful and fidgety half hour worrying about his upcoming task. At six o'clock Ned was stepping into his shower and, as he began his personal hygiene preparations for the night ahead, broke into song – "They all laughed at Christopher Columbus when he said the world was round. They all laughed when Edison recorded sound."

Before Dobson had got to the third verse Prosser was heading out of the Plaza's front door and across the road to the Tivoli Gardens with a blue and white bag, unaware of its illegal contents. Being caught in possession of a kilo of cocaine would take an awful lot of explaining. Jack Prosser was not blessed with even a fraction of the guile needed just to make a stab at it.

While Prosser was trying to get to grips with Tivoli's entrance fee in its strange currency Vaughan Ames was checking in at the Plaza's reception desk. The hotels receptionist for the evening had just come on shift. He was a young and fit looking Dane with short blond hair and had that permanently tanned look that all Scandinavians seem to be born with. The young man smiled politely as he handed Ames his key.

"Your room is on the fourth floor Sir. Would you like a hand with your luggage to your room?"

Ames felt he saw a twinkle in the lads bright blue eyes as he made the offer. The town must be full of perverts, he thought. No wonder Wynstanly and Dobson came here.

"Your luggage sir. Do you require any assistance?" The young man repeated.

"NO! Er! No thank you. I've only got an overnight bag with me. Oh! by the way I believe you have some friends of mine staying here. A Mr. Wynstanly and a Mr. Dobson. Is that correct?"

"Mr Dobson. Yes sir, but not Mr. Wynstanly. The other gentleman who came with Mr. Dobson was a Mr. Prosser. Their rooms are on the third floor, 373 and 386 sir."

PROSSER! Ames thought for a moment. So, Wynstanly has booked himself in under a false name. Trying to cover his tracks. Well don't worry Denzil old chap. By this time next week the whole of the County of Gloucestershire will know about you and your unnatural perversion.

In the shower of room 373 Ned was bringing an imaginary audience in a packed Carnegie Hall to a peak of adulation. Tommy Dorsie's musicians were giving it all they got.

"Ho Ho Ho – Who's got the last laugh? Ha Ha Ha – Who's got the last laugh? Hey Hey Hey – Who's got the last laugh – now?"

Tucking a large towel over the top of his bulging beer belly he stepped out of the bathroom. He noticed a folded piece of paper that had been pushed under his door. He picked it up, sat on the side of the bed and read the message it contained.

THEY WERE WATCHING YOU THIS AFTERNOON. BE CAREFUL. COME TO MAXINE'S BAR ON COLBJORNSENSGADE TONIGHT AT EIGHT THIRTY. I WILL MAKE MYSELF KNOWN TO YOU WHEN I AM SURE YOU WERE NOT FOLLOWED.

Ned scratched his belly and read the note again.

What's this crap about? WATCHING YOU THIS AFTERNOON? I'm a bloody reporter. There's no law against interviewing people on the street. Denmark is not a police state? Ned shrugged his bare shoulders and began to screw the strange note up. It didn't make sense anyway. The idea that the Danish football team had been handed the European Championship as a reward for turning in a YES vote on Maastricht was just a joke that he had thought up to get off Denzil's hook. Prosser was the only other person who was in on it.

So, either Prosser had shoved the note under the door himself to put him off, or –!!

"Bugger me," Ned shouted out loud. "Bloody buggery buggery." He said again as if he hadn't heard himself the first time. "Somebody DID do a deal with the Danes. I am on to something. Something BIG – bugger me. BIG! BIG!"

He unscrewed the note and with his Plaza Hotel bath towel round his waist took off down the corridor in the direction of Prosser's room. His mind was racing. Who was in on it? The Germans? The French? The Brits? Or the whole bloody lot of them. Who was the brains behind the plot? Ned would have given his right testicle to know. If anyone had offered him confirmation that Randolph was involved he would have briefly considered sacrificing both.

Hotel bedroom doors all look the same. Had Ned been able to recover some control over his racing mind as he ran down the corridor he would have remembered that Prosser was in room 386. In his excitement at being on to the biggest story of his journalistic life he stopped one door too soon and began hammering on the door of room number 384.

"Prosser," Ned called, hopping up and down. "Open up. Look at this." And he held up the piece of paper as if it were visible through the solid timber door.

Ned's elation at his belief that he was onto the scoop of the century was boundless. It consumed him totally. And in its total consumption he failed to notice that he was getting an erection. For the first time since Gwendolyn had kicked him in the balls he was getting a fair to middling stiffy. Percy had woken from his pain induced sleep and was now wide awake and ready for some action.

Vaughan Ames had just reached the landing on the third floor when he heard a voice in the corridor to his left, an excited voice and one that was not unknown to him.

Dobson! – what's he up to?

Ames edged along the wall and slowly stuck his head round the corner to get a look. The sight confronting him caused his eyes to widen and his mouth to open. Dobson was hopping up and down on a bath towel, hammering on a bedroom door completely naked and with a hard on that looked as though it could drill a hole in concrete.

"Open up. I've got something to show you. This one's a whopper."

Ames could not believe his eyes. He pulled back took a couple of deep breaths and peeped round the corner for confirmation. Sure enough. The Record's political, social and environmental correspondent was trying to break down his gay lover's bedroom door with his dick. What a story. Who would believe it – got to get it on film – the camera quick.

Ames dropped to his knees unzipped his blue and white S.A.S. bag and took out his camera. Keeping himself out of sight he pushed the camera out into the corridor and fired off three or four shots. Retrieving the camera he lent back against the wall.

"Got him the dirty little wretch. Round one to the Clarion."

Room 384 at the Plaza Hotel was occupied by Elmer and Sadie Wienburger. Elmer and Sadie had flown in from Dallas that morning on the first leg of their European tour. They were sleeping after their long and tiresome flight. Elmer Wienburger was stretched out on the bed in a pair of blue silk Dallas Cowboys boxer shorts. Next to him Sadie was gently snoring. Her bulbous breasts and belly rose and fell with each breath like a rhythmical Atlantic swell. Sadie was wearing a white see-through chiffon neck to ankle nightdress plus – Mimi. A matching white miniature French poodle. A real, live, white, miniature French poodle, tucked lovingly under Sadie's arm. Daytime or night time Mimi went everywhere tucked under Sadie's arm. Mimi the poodle and Sadie were inseparable. There would be no Grand European Tour unless Elmer could fix it that Mimi could come too. Elmer fixed it.

Mimi never walked anywhere. The animal's feet never touched the ground except when she was required to do her duty. Whenever Mimi felt the ground under her feet she knew instinctively what she had to do.

The commotion outside their hotel room door had woken the Wienbergers from their sleep.

"Did you order room service?" Elmer drawled sleepily. "Get the door willya."

Mimi, remained tucked under Sadie's arm as she hurried to carry out Elmer's instructions. The commotion was maybe some sort of Danish fire drill so she abandoned her usual precaution of keeping the door on the security chain and flung it open. Whether Ned was more shocked than Sadie will forever be a matter of debate at the Tip.

HE saw a large, ghost like, toothless, female form. It was wearing a purple headband and a see-through night-dress that left no room for even the smallest of imaginations. Its face was covered in a white cream. Another face, the elfin like face of a strange looking animal was peeping out from under the apparition's armpit.

SHE was shocked to a momentary standstill by the sight of a naked man stood on a bath towel with an erection pointing in the general direction of the orifice where her teeth would normally be residing. Both fell backwards on to their respective floors.

Ned recovered first. Grabbing his towel from the floor, he took off for his room. Sadie remained flat on her back, screaming with every outward breath that her monolithic lungs could expel, flailing her legs and cellulite about in a most unladylike manner.

Mimi, the poodle, upon feeling her feet touch the ground, had a crap and a pee before burrowing under Sadie's night-dress in canine confusion.

Elmer was now off the bed. "What the blue hell is going on?"

From his position seated on the floor of the landing of the Plaza hotel Vaughan Ames now heard a different commotion. A women screaming, a man shouting and a dog barking.

"It's a bloody orgy! And with animals!"

He poked his head round the corner. There was no sign of Dobson but the door of 384 was open and all hell appeared to have broken out. Ames crawled on his hands and knees until he reached the door. Once again he pushed his camera forward and fired off another four shots before retreating to the safety of his room.

Vaughan Ames placed his bag on the bed, sat down and considered his next move. True, he had caught Dobson dancing naked in a public place and even had photographic evidence. His camera also held the secrets of the noisy commotion that was going on just inside the door of room 384. But the voices were not familiar and he had not actually heard or seen Wynstanly or – "Prosser", if that was what he was calling himself whilst here in Copenhagen. Fornicating under an assumed name would not make the deed any less newsworthy to the Clarion's loyal and morally upright readers. He now knew that Dobson was still in the hotel but was Wynstanly? He picked up the telephone and dialled reception.

"Do you know if Mr. er Prosser is still in the hotel?"

"No sir. Mr. Prosser left the hotel just a few moments ago."

"Oh dear! That is a pity. I wanted to speak with him. Did he say how long he would be out for?"

"He didn't say, sir. He asked for directions to the bandstand at Tivoli. I believe he was meeting someone there, sir"

Vaughan Ames replaced the receiver, checked his camera for film, returned it to the blue and white bag which he hung over his shoulder and headed for Copenhagen's Tivoli Gardens. As he passed the Plaza's reception desk a few late arrivals were waiting to be checked in. Ames paid them no attention as he left the hotel. Not even to the vicar who's only luggage was an identical blue and white bag.

The hotel receptionist handed Rhys Howells his room key but before the Reverend could inquire as to the whereabouts of Mr Dobson the man himself came bounding down the stairs.

The unexpected sight of the vicar standing in the foyer of Copenhagen's Plaza hotel phased Ned for a moment.

But he had recovered from his frightful encounter with the gruesome Sadie Wienburger, and was back to full journalistic stimulation at being on the trail of a huge international scoop. The Plaza's cleaner was also on the trail of an international scoop. The one which Mimi the poodle had left behind and which Elmer had trodden in and trailed back into the bedroom whilst trying to comfort his distraught wife.

"Hells Bells vicar! What are you doing here? On a mission are you? The Red Light district is behind the train station if that's where you're heading. Plenty of souls need saving down there eh! Nice suit pal. See you later."

"No! Stop! Stop! Mr. Dobson. It's not the girls I'm after tonight – that is to say – it's you I need to talk to."

Ned had to try and find Prosser and be at Maxine's in an hour to meet someone who had information that could make him Journalist of the Year. They would then be free to spend the rest of the night boozing and letching on Wynstanly's credit card. Nattering to a vicar was not on the night's agenda.

"Can't stop now vicar, I've got to find the Birdman –"

"The Bird Man?"

"Yes! The Birdman – Jack Prosser. You know – oh well! maybe you don't. Anyway he's out there somewhere and I need to find him quick like."

"Mr. Prosser has gone over to the Tivoli Gardens sir"

"Eh!" Ned looked across at the hotel receptionist. "Oh! cheers, thanks, right, I'm off then see you in the morning vicar, not too early mind, we're not planning on getting in much before dawn."

"No! No! Stop again Mr. Dobson." The Reverend Howells was now following Ned through the Plaza's revolving door out into the street.

They were both halfway across Bernstorffsgade dodging the oncoming cars and buses when; "It's Randolph Mr. Dobson, Randolph Fors-Bowers. He wants to talk to you. I believe he wants to make it up

133

with you before he – well I got the impression that he hasn't got long to – er live."

Ned stopped in his tracks.

Neither he nor Rhys Howells spotted the approaching cyclist who had to swerve sharply to avoid the two men who had stopped so suddenly in front of him. The cyclist managed to miss them but clipped the edge of an oncoming bus just enough to send him careering into the dozens of bicycles parked outside the train station.

Ned grabbed the vicar by the lapels of his new light grey summer suit. They were both, oblivious to the accident they had just caused as well as the traffic that was rushing passed on both sides.

"You mean I've cracked it with that old bugger at last? He's about to peg it and leave me half of Wiltshire as a going away present. When man? When do I get my hands on his – er! When do I get to see him? I must make my last, fond, goodbyes to the old gentleman."

"Mr Fors-Bowers has sent me with explicit instructions to bring you back as soon as possible, immediately in fact."

"Hmm," Ned thought for a moment. "How about the first plane out in the morning? Only, I've got to find Prosser first, then meet someone who is going to pass me some pretty useful info on a news story that I'm on to."

"Mr. Fors-Bowers would be happy to see you back in the country by tomorrow, I'm sure. We shall get an early plane out of Copenhagen. In the meantime, if you would be good enough to let go of my lapels, this suit is quite new and was quite expensive. The parish stipend hardly covers my living expenses. I have had to live quite frugally in order to save enough money for its purchase."

Ned released his grip and smoothed the suit back into shape. He suspected that the vicar's hint at penury may have been a reminder of the financial reward that he had been promised. Vicar Howells could hint from now until judgement day. Once Ned had got his hands on

Randolph's estate the vicar would be abandoned. He would have to sing for his supper in someone else's choir.

"Right then vicar. You pop back to the hotel and have a glass of holy water, or whatever it is you vicars drink for a night-cap, and we'll see you in the morning."

"Could I not come with you? I have little else to do this evening and I have never yet had the pleasure of seeing a top newspaper reporter at work."

"You can if you like vicar, but Prosser and me are heading for Maxine's Bar and – well er! the girls there, the dancers that is, don't exactly wear too many clothes. In fact one or two of them have been known to strip off completely."

The Reverend Rhys Howells perked up at this graphic description of the sort of entertainment on show at Maxine's Bar. His interest was all too obvious by the rising colour in his cheeks.

"As a man of the cloth, Mr. Dobson, I regard it as my solemn duty to put my personal feelings to one side and take the Word to the seamiest of iniquitous dens. Those poor girls are simply lost souls in need of a direction and I intend to give them one. Take me to Maxine's Bar – I insist."

"You're on Vicar, but let's get off this road before we get run over. We'll grab Prosser from the Tivoli then I'll take you to Maxine's and you can direct as many girls as you can lay your hands on, clerically speaking of course."

After a lifetime spent permanently under the cosh Edward Dobson now believed that Lady Luck was about to reward him. First with a spell of journalistic stardom and thereafter to a life of opulent ease as the new squire of the Fors-Bowers estate.

Oh dear! The coupling of arrogance to greed can render a chap quite blind at times.

17

Jan Ericsson was the Corporate Manager of Euro-Scan, a cable television company that relayed adult films and programmes to the more liberal minded Europeans. Ericsson was based in Gothenburg, Sweden, where part of his duties were to lay on extravagant hospitality for visiting T.V. bosses, Politicians and Chiefs of Police. In fact for anyone who his boss and owner of Euro-Scan, Hans Krog, sent him to entertain.

Krog had spent many years and much money on generating lasting friendships with influential and powerful people. In return these connections had often felt obliged to open a door or two for Krog and his ever-expanding business empire.

It must come as no surprise to learn, therefore, that Krog was also a ruthless and demanding employer. That morning, Ericsson had received orders direct from Krog himself. The orders were simple enough but as they had come to him via Krog's private telephone Ericsson knew that they had to be carried out to perfection. Ericsson's first task was to draw one hundred thousand pounds sterling from the company's corporate account at the Den Danske bank. He must place the cash in a blue and white Scandinavian Air System's flight bag and at precisely 7 p.m. that evening be at the bandstand in the Tivoli Gardens. Here he would make contact with a British visitor carrying an identical bag which would contain the company's monthly requirement of corporate cocaine. The supply must then be handed to Krog personally that evening. Hans Krog trusted no-one, not even one of his highest and trusted managers. It was unusual for Ericsson to be put at risk in this way. The regular front line dealer would normally be the one to carry out this task, but

Ericsson had been in the employment of Krog long enough to know when not to ask the reasons why. Before his 7 p.m. appointment at the Tivoli Ericsson had one other task-order from Krog. He was required to follow and watch two newspaper reporters who had arrived in Copenhagen that day from England. These two men, Krog had said, were getting too close. If they tried to get any nearer to the Krog business they had to be stopped. When Hans Krog said that someone had to be stopped he meant stopped – DEAD.

That morning Ericsson had picked up the two men outside the airport and followed them, first to the Plaza and then to Parliament Square. The blue and white bag, slung over his shoulder holding the cash, helped him to look casual. Throughout the afternoon he had copied Ned's and Prosser's every move as ordered even matching them lager for lager. After all, they were just a couple of Englishmen, what would they know of the perils of consuming large quantities of Danish premium lager?

Ericsson just managed to contact his assistant Lars at his Gothenburg office before he passed out, sprawled across the table outside Sam's bistro. He regained consciousness around 6.30 p.m. His face red with sunburn, his mobile phone missing, presumed stolen from the table where he had left it. Fortunately, the blue and white flight bag containing one hundred thousand pounds of the Krog Empire's cash remained beneath his head where he had been using it as a pillow.

The mobile phone could be replaced. Sadly the message on it, from his ruthless employer, demanding that Ericsson contact him immediately, could not. Ericsson would have been told that Krog had urgent business in Brussels. The deal was off until Saturday.

Jan Ericsson, high flying Corporate Manager to Krog's Euro-Scan Empire was, like Jack Prosser, ignorant to the fact that the appointment at the Tivoli had now been postponed for two days. Believing that he had less than twenty minutes to get to the Tivoli and that taxis at that time in the evening would be hard to come by, he stole a bike from the many that were parked outside Sam's Bistro and took off for the Gardens.

Jan Ericsson was fit. He worked out at the company's fitness centre each morning. The bike that he had stolen was old, heavy and not designed for speed. But with Ericsson's powerful thighs pumping at the pedals it touched speeds that its makers would never have thought possible. He crossed Hans Christian Andersen Boulevard, down Tietgensgade before turning right into Bernstorffsgade and the side entrance to Tivoli that he had been told his contact would be using.

He had no physical description of the man he was looking for. The only information he had was that his man would be British and carrying a bag identical to the one now slung over his own shoulder.

He sped down the middle of the road and was about to slow down and cross over to the right hand side and the entrance to Tivoli when he suddenly spotted two pedestrians standing in his path. As he swerved to avoid them the last thing he remembered was that one of them was dressed as a vicar and carrying a blue and white bag identical to the one that was on his own shoulder.

The accident had left Ericsson dazed and concussed with a stream of blood running down the side of his face from a cut above his left eyebrow. His grey, Brodene Anderson tailor made suit was a write off. It's right hand pocket now hung limply, held on only by the bottom stitching. Both knees of the trousers were ripped. What was once a creaseless blue shirt was oil stained and torn and now exposed an under garment. A black T shirt with the words The Copenhagen Connection printed in large white letters.

His head was pounding as he tried to disentangle himself from the pile of bikes that he was enmeshed in. People were coming over to help him. Their faces swimming and dancing in front of his eyes. Across the street he could just pick out the man with the identical bag pushing through the Tivoli turnstiles. This must be his contact, disguised as a vicar. Good, who would suspect a vicar? It was to be his last lucid thought for that evening.

Every time he tried to stand up the bike he had been riding came up with him. His brown and cream patterned tie was firmly wrapped around the chain. Help, however, was not too far away. An elderly lady kneeling on the pavement was rummaging, head and hands, inside a large shopping bag. She eventually emerged, triumphantly brandishing a pair of scissors. The concussed Ericsson made no murmur of dissent as she picked her way through the bent and twisted cycles and, with one quick snip set him free. Without offering even a grunt of thanks he picked up the bag with the cash and staggered off.

Moments later a taxi pulled up outside the entrance. Frankie Ferranti paid the driver and hurried into the Gardens. From Gloucester to Heathrow to Copenhagen to the Tivoli Gardens Frankie had The Voice's words continually ringing in his ears.

"Frankie, my sweet Italian pomegranate, if I cannot rely on you then who, who am I to turn to? You are the one, my olive skinned Adonis. Postpone the deal for a mere two days and you shall have anything your heart desires."

The Voice's unspoken words were 'mess it up and your heart will desire a body to live in.'

So concerned was he to placate his powerful master that Frankie's own survival instincts had, for the moment, lost their edge. He failed to notice that his taxi had been followed from the airport by a dark blue BMW saloon. As Ferranti's taxi pulled away the saloon glided to a halt in the vacated space. Two casually dressed men got out from the back of the car. One of them looked across the street towards the railway station and nodded to another, leaning against the station wall. This third man radioed a message.

An officer in charge of two cars full of armed Danish policemen and the pilot of a police helicopter circling the city to the east of Tivoli received the message.

"Frankie Ferranti has entered The Gardens."

18

Jack Prosser was now inside Tivoli. The evening was warm and sultry, the end of an unusually hot Scandinavian day. A wind was getting up, indicating a change in the mid-summer weather. Storm clouds and strong winds were coming in from southern Europe. Jack Prosser had little interest in the latest weather forecast.

He had less than ten minutes to get to the bandstand, find the man with a blue and white bag, the same as his, then make a swap. What if there was more than one person carrying a blue and white flight bag? These bags were not uncommon. People on holiday would use them to carry their bits around. What if grey suits and black shirts were the fashion in Denmark? What if he picked on the wrong one? There would be an argument, with a stranger, probably in a foreign language. The 'what ifs' were causing him to break out in a sweat. The front of his own shirt was already sticking to his chest. Behind him a steady stream of visitors were coming in through the Bernstorffsgade entrance. Similar numbers entered through the Glypotek Group entrance on Hans Christian Andersen Boulevard. At Tivoli's majestic main entrance on Vesterbrogade the crowds were pouring in. The directions he had recieved from the Plaza's receptionist were a jumble in his racing mind. He tried to pick out the way to the bandstand from a Tivoli guide book. He was being jostled and nudged by hordes of fun seeking Danes and foreign visitors all out for a good time. The printed guide informed him that since the Gardens opened in 1843 more than 260 million people had passed through it's turnstiles. In his increasing tense and anxious state Jack Prosser felt that the whole lot of them had turned up that evening, just to make it even more difficult for him. At last he spotted a sign post directing him to the bandstand.

"There he goes!" Ned caught sight of Prosser's mop of wiry, grey hair bobbing its way through the crowds. The tall angular form of his mate was unmistakable.

Ned barged his way through the crowds in the direction that he had seen Prosser heading. "Out the way – Out the way – Coming through – get out the bloody way will you."

A few moments of abusive barging and shoving and he realised that he'd lost, not only, Prosser but also the vicar. He turned around and could just see the hairless head of the diminutive cleric struggling to make his way.

"Excuse me – so sorry may I get by – thank you so much – I beg your pardon – may I ..."

"Come on vicar put your skates on. I've lost him. I reckon he went this way, come on."

Ned and the vicar made their way through the crowds until they arrived at a an open space in front of the main concert hall.

"Right! Hold up. Let's stop for a minute. I'm sure he was heading this way."

"Who did you say we are looking for?"

"The Birdman." Ned answered curtly. "Jack Prosser – studies birds and takes photos for the Record. You know – I told you – we are on an assignment – for Wynstanly – remember? In your kitchen?"

"Ah! Yes I remember now. But as I have never met Mr. Prosser I have no idea what he looks like."

"Oh! Right. Well he's tall, grey haired got hands like shovels and is probably wearing a white open necked shirt with the sleeves rolled up, a pair of brown trousers and brown shoes – not exactly a martyr to fashion so he should stick out like a sore thumb amongst this lot."

The Aldo Niels-Sloberg, Tribute to Glen Miller, band had just settled into their seats on the stage of Tivoli's bandstand. Aldo's musicians were dressed in stone grey shirts and trousers and neatly tied beige ties. Every pair of black shoes on parade that evening were highly polished. Those musicians who had hair wore crew cuts. All were clean shaven. The band was seated on a rising platform. In the front line were four trombones, behind them four sax players with an assortment of tenor and alto saxophones. The lead saxophone player also played clarinet. Sat behind the reed section were four trumpet players. At the top, on the left hand side, were the rhythm and chords section, a drummer, double bass player, guitarist and pianist.

Their leader was more formally dressed as a Major of the American Air Force. He wore a pair of stylish, rimless glasses. As he turned to smile a slow enigmatic smile at his audience they knew that beneath his peaked cap would be a mop of black wavy hair. He held a trombone in his left hand and he acknowledged the enthusiastic applause of the large crowd of big band fans.

If his well turned out ensemble of talented musicians were the embodiment of Major Glen Miller's orchestra, of the 30's and 40's, then Aldo Niels-Sloberg WAS the great man himself – reincarnate.

Aldo lived and breathed Miller. He had scored his band's music exactly as Miller would have done. Every bar was note perfect. Not a minim or dotted crochet out of place. There was nothing that Aldo did not know about the music and life of Glen Miller.

Aldo smiled at the crowd seated on the benches in front of him and turned towards the band.

"We'll start with No. 6."

Overhead the clouds were thickening and the distant rumblings of a thunderstorm could be heard. The wind was increasing to the point where some of the musicians felt obliged to make use of small plastic pegs to hold the pages of their music in place. Others trusted the thin metal arms of their music stands.

"Are we ready then? One – Two – One Two Three Four."

With absolute precision, and precisely at nineteen hundred hours Central European Time, the drummer marched the band into Aldo's faultless arrangement of St. Louis Blues.

As he made his way towards the bandstand Frankie Ferranti spotted a tall, grey haired, well dressed gentleman in the crowd and walking away from him. The man was carrying a bag which appeared to be identical to the one he had given to Sophie containing a kilo of the cocaine that the 'The Voice' had left for him at the golf club. The man was obviously looking for someone or, possibly something. The Tivoli bandstand for instance. Could this be Jack Prosser?

Sophie's description of the Record's photographer was almost perfect except that even from a distance this man looked immaculately dressed. The impression that Frankie had was more of a rustic person than the one who had just turned around and was now facing him with a look of astonishment on his face that mirrored his own.

"Mr. Ames!!!" Frankie could scarcely get the name out.

"Ferranti! What are you doing here?"

For a moment Frankie Ferranti held his breath. He quickly regained his composure. There was too much at stake to start fumbling for words now.

"Oh! A short holiday break Mr. Ames. And Copenhagen is probably my most favourite city – next to my hometown of Florence of course. A beautiful place don't you think? But of course you must or you would not be here yourself. A holiday for you as well perhaps? A break from the rigours of reporting the world's news?" Frankie machine-gunned the words out as a cover for his confusion. A confusion which changed to suspicion when –.

"No not a holiday at all. In fact I am over here on newspaper business. I heard that two of the Record's staff were over here. We believe that they are onto something. It doesn't pay to let your rivals get too far ahead of you in this business."

He knows. Frankie thought. Someone has tipped him

off. Touber maybe? Ames' golfing partner. The Chief Inspector had been after Frankie's tail for months. On his home patch, the police were no match for the clever Italian. Frankie Ferranti always covered his tracks as immaculately as he dressed.

But here was not Gloucestershire, here was Copenhagen. Here he was on strange ground and forced by circumstances to get involved in a situation that he would normally stay well away from.

Ferranti knew that Vaughan Ames's paper The Clarion, just as Wynstanly's Record, reported only local news. News that hardly got further than the top of the Cotswold Hills. But if either one of the papers ran a story of a drugs bust in the Capital City of Denmark there was a chance that it would reach one of the nationals. If he, Frankie Ferranti, was found to be caught up in this turnover then his operation in England would collapse. His hopes of promotion within The Voice's organisation would dissolve quicker than a jab of whiz in a glass of lager.

Another thought struck him harder than the thunderbolts in the storm coming up from the south. If, indeed, Touber does know that there is something going down here in Tivoli then the place will be crawling with Danish police. AND he, Frankie Ferranti, is at this moment talking to a tall grey haired man carrying a bag identical to the two bags. One holding a delivery of drugs and the other 100,000 pounds Stirling. He had no doubt that they were being watched right at that moment.

PANIC! He had to get away from Ames and out of Tivoli fast.

PANIC! Tivoli is enclosed and only has three exits. They will all be blocked by the police.

PANIC! He was – TRAPPED!.

WAIT! What a fool he was. He did not have to leave Ames. Ames was his way out. Ames had a blue and white bag yes!, but what was in it? A change of clothes – a toilet bag – a note pad – tape recorder – a camera –

newspaper man's paraphernalia nothing more. What could be more natural than two old friends, members of the same golf club even, meeting and socialising on a short holiday. A rumble of thunder concentrated his racing mind.

"Mr. Ames, you must allow me to buy you dinner. I thought you took your unexpected defeat on the golf course yesterday with great dignity." Lie! – Wynstanly, Tauber and even Frankie himself could see that Ames was seething with indignation at being beaten that day. "The rest of this, ungentlemanly, world could learn great lessons in sportsmanship from the British. You must allow me to buy you dinner. I would be honoured."

Every one of us, whether we care to admit it or not, enjoys praise. Even when it is such obvious, bum licking, praise as that which Frankie had just tongued Ames with. We still want to hear it, feel it. It is another fact that if the praise, or bum licking, comes from someone we dislike, detest even, then by some perverse quirk of human nature the lick feels all the more pleasurable for it.

Vaughen Ames was set back on his heels at this unexpected outburst of laudation coming form the Italian. But he was not the first and, would not be the last male, or female, to be beguiled by Ferranti's cunning.

"Well! That's very kind of you But I really must find Mr. Wynst – er – Mr. Prosser or I will lose the chance of my share of the news that is about to break."

If it was possible to frown inwardly then the inside of Frankie's face would be covered with the lines of an inverse look of complete displeasure. Prosser! Ames was looking for PROSSER the very man than he Frankie Ferranti had sent here with a bag containing, what he could only now think of as, his entire future. He must not let Ames out of his sight – not let him go anywhere near the bandstand. ANYWHERE near Jack Prosser.

"Mr. Ames. Mr. Ames? How formal that sounds.

Adversaries we may be on the golf course but off it, and especially here in this friendly city of Copenhagen, we two must also be friends. Please allow me to address you by your Christian name – Vaughan is it not? – such a distinguished sounding name for such a distinguished gentleman. And you must call me Frankie or Francesco if you prefer – I shall leave it up to you. My friend, finding your Mr. Prosser here in Tivoli will be like looking for a needle in a haystack. Please, again, I ask you to join me for dinner. There are many excellent restaurants here in Tivoli. I shall take you to the Balkan, it is a fine place. Listen! there is a storm coming. The clouds are darkening, the wind is getting stronger by the minute. If your friend is here in Tivoli and the storm breaks then there is a chance that he will take shelter and eat in the very same restaurant. You will kill two birds with one stone – enjoy a pleasant evening – meet your man AND get your story. AH! Mathematics was never my strongest attribute – I believe that came to three birds. Come! This way. The food here is fantastic."

* * *

"ALL UNITS! ALL UNITS! – FERRANTI AND ONE BAG ARE HEADING FOR THE BALKAN – ONE BAG ALREADY AT THE BANDSTAND TWO MORE APPROACHING FROM DIFFERENT DIRECTIONS – GET THE HELICOPTOR UP WE WILL NEED SEARCHLIGHTS – IT IS GETTING DARK – THE WEATHER IS CLOSING IN – COVER ALL EXITS – STANDBY"

* * *

Even a concussed Jan Ericsson was no stranger to Tivoli. On entering the Bernstorffsgade gate he lurched and staggered towards the bandstand, driven on by the spectre of Krog administering his own particular kind of punishment for failure. The blood from the cut above his eye had now dried, leaving a dark red scar running from eyebrow to lower chin. The knees and one jacket pocket of his once perfectly fitted suit flapped in unison with his stride. His battered and dishevelled appearance drew curious glances from the more inquisitive of Tivoli's evening revellers.

He did not immediately join the assembled gathering of music lovers seated on the benches in front of the stage. Instead he positioned himself to the right of the stage facing the audience and lent behind one of the many trees that populated the Gardens. His head was thumping and his vision was beginning to blur. A tall, grey haired man was standing at the back of the audience carrying a blue and white bag. Ericsson could just make out that it was one of the two men he had been asked to watch that afternoon. Now, confusion and suspicion filled his aching head.

Where did he get the bag? Did he steal it from the vicar, his contact? Has he stolen the bag containing the drugs that he had been charged by his employer to bring safely and intact back to Gothenburg. Remembering Krog's instructions to 'stop them if they got too close' he slipped his bruised hand inside his tattered jacket and unclipped the holster that held his loaded Berreta.

Jack Prosser's pale green eyes searched the crowd, anxiously looking for anyone carrying a bag the same as his. Blue and white. Blue and white. His eyes were used to spotting much less obvious colours and much more cleverly camouflaged. He could spot the brown, plumage of the tiny Tree-Creeper clinging to the trunk of a tree from ten metres. He had a beautiful photograph of a Nightjar, a bird more often heard than seen. But these sightings were made in his other life where he was Birdman Jack Prosser, easy-going and unhurried. Today in this place, this foreign place, he was Bag-swap Jack Prosser, edgy, nervous and far from his natural habitat. He wanted to get this over quickly, grab the other bag dump it in his room, then persuade Ned to find a quiet pub where the pair of them could sit and drink. Ned could natter on as much as he wanted to. He would just sit quietly puffing on his pipe, pretending to listen. It may not be as good as the Tip but it would be good enough.

Unlucky Jack! This is swinging Copenhagen not sleepy Monks End and Ned has other plans.

St Louis Blues was now getting the full treatment from Aldo's band of devoted Miller muso's. The brasses were hammering out the top line with gusto supremo. Trombones and trumpets swinging from side to side in measured arcs. The crowd were equally excited and showed their appreciation by clapping, more or less in time, with the music. The atmosphere at the Tivoli bandstand was happy and getting happier by the second. Not quite electric, that would come later.

"Hey! Jacko you old bugger. There you are."

Jack instantly recognised the voice and the greeting. However, when he turned around his eyes focused on, not his mate Ned, or on the other man with him but on the blue and white bag that the other man was carrying.

"Jacko! Jacko! The vicar here's got some great news. He's come over from Glos. Randolph's capitulated mate, caved in, wants me back tomorrow to make it up. I knew I'd get him in the end. I'm gonna be rich pal. Lord of the manor, Squire Ned. One of the landed gentry. What d'you reckon?

"Oh! er! Great!"

What Jack Prosser really reckoned, was that this vicar had not come over from Glos – Gloucester to tell Ned that Randolph wanted him. That must be just a bluff. This vicar was wearing a light grey suit and a black shirt. His jacket was done up so Jack couldn't tell if there was any writing on it. But, it WAS black and he did have a blue and white bag. This must be the man he had to swap bags with. WHY this vicar had brought his bag from Gloucester, just as he had done WHY they both had to go back to Gloucester carrying different bags to the ones they brought were questions that didn't concern him. The only questions Jack Prosser wanted answering were; how he could change bags with this vicar without Ned catching on? and, how quick could he get out of this place and into a local for a quiet pint?

If Prosser had been a churchgoer the phrase 'Divine Intervention' may have had some meaning. But Jack Prosser wasn't and it didn't. When Rhys Howells handed Jack his blue and white bag to hold, whilst he bent down to tie a shoelace loosened by the hurrying and scurrying through Tivoli, Birdman Jack Prosser took it to be a simple sign from the earthly vicar himself.

Jan Ericsson's head was pounding. Any doctor worth his over paid salt would have instantly diagnosed severe concussion. The result of the bang received when Jan had collided with the cluster of bicycles outside the railway station. The pounding in his head was not being helped by the thump thump thump of the blades of a helicopter hovering above Tivoli. Ericsson had just enough control over his diminishing faculties to spot the swapping of bags that Prosser had just executed. The tall, craggy, grey haired guy is now definitely stealing Hans Krog's grade 'A' Colombian which his boss had commanded him to bring 'safely and intact' back to Gothenburg.

Ericsson produced the Berreta from under his tattered jacket and took an unsteady aim at Jack Prosser's head.

A sudden clap of thunder brought an OOH! from the audience. It also masked the sound of the crack from Ericssons' gun. The bullet was heading straight for the temple of Jack Prosser's skull. Fortunately, Ericsson's grasp of the finer points of the delivery of a classic piece of 40's Miller, was less than the intelligence quotient of a grain of sand. He pressed the trigger the instant the lead trombone had arched his instrument. The bullet took the merest of deflections off the slide of the trombone and entered the front of the bag hanging over Rhys Howell's shoulder. It silently tore its way through the contents, leaving a gaping hole in the bottom of the bag before embedding itself into the ground.

The thunder and the increasing velocity of the wind combined to leave vicar Howells oblivious to the impact of the bullet on the bag that he was carrying. The consequences, however, became all too clear when a stream of white powder began to fall from the bottom of the bag.

Very little of it reached the ground. The wind whipped it up and passed it on and into the respiratory systems of the audience, musicians, Prosser, Ned, Howells, Ericsson, indeed, anyone who happened to be within snorting distance.

In less than half a minute a whole kilo of Hans Krog's cocaine had been inhaled by the assembled crowd.

Ericsson could not understand how the bag that should have had the stuff was – there, and the bag that shouldn't have had the stuff was – there, and now the stuff was – everywhere. He fired again and missed, again. This time his shot was heard. The band stopped playing the audience ducked and crouched among the benches. The helicopter came lower, its searchlight panned backwards and forwards until it picked out the gunman.

"THERE HE IS."

Police sirens wailed and a loud hailer barked out.

"PUT DOWN YOUR WEAPON – YOU ARE SURROUNDED – YOU ARE SURROUNDED."

Ericsson, wild eyed, dishevelled and totally disorientated made to fire again. A volley of shots flew over the heads of the crowd. Some embedded themselves in the tree that he was stood behind and some zinged passed his ears. The helicopter's blades were thumping the air above the crowd. Any residue of Colombian marching powder that had failed to enter nostrils was whipped up for a second snort.

Another crack. This time a thunderbolt of electricity from the heavens. A huge clap of thunder rattled the windows of the Balkan restaurant and large drops of rain started falling from the blackened sky.

Amplified demands mingled with sirens and thunder. "YOU ARE SURROUNDED – PUT DOWN YOUR WEAPON – SURRENDER NOW."

Surrender? Never. Ericsson charged over the crouching crowd, stepping on hands, heads and benches swinging his own bag and firing wildly upwards, sideways, straight ahead. He hurled his own cash filled bag at the prostrate figures of Ned, Prosser and the vicar. In one, final act of confused desperation he snatched the bag from Howells and ran of. As he ran away it puffed lesser quantities of white powder from the hole in its bottom. A dozen or more armed policemen emerged from the bushes and chased him through the crowds of amazed revellers.

At the sounds of gunfire Aldo's first feelings were not of fright but of annoyance. His concert tribute to his all time musical hero, Glen Miller, had been suddenly interrupted. Worse, the band had been forced to stop playing St Louis Blues when there were still six bars to go. As he knelt down on one knee, brushing a white powdery substance from his tunic, his annoyance suddenly changed to elation. This feeling grew and grew until a great surge of energy filled his body. He was no longer Aldo Neils-Sloberg, he was Glen Miller. It was war time London. He could hear the bombs falling, wailing air raid sirens and gun fire. A crazed German spy had been flushed out and was being chased through Hyde Park. Now his audience needed a lift to be reminded of the good things of the world. He would raise these Londoner's spirits. He knew exactly what he had to do. Aldo stood up, turned to his band, and raised his baton. Taking their cue from their leader, the musicians regained their composure, picked up their instruments and waited for his instructions. There could only be one tune to call.

"Number one please. We will play number one."

The reed and brass sections stood. The saxophonists placed their instruments to their mouths and, on the down beat of Aldo's baton, threw themselves into a hair-raising version of 'In the Mood', Miller's unmistakable signature tune.

The effect on the crowd was as instant as the hit they had just received from the cocaine. With a roar they rose to their feet. Shouting, clapping, cheering, dancing on the ground and on the benches. The rain turned into a downpour. Thunder, lightning, searchlights, sirens and gunfire combined to heighten their feelings of ecstatic euphoria.

As the rain increased so some people started to take off their clothes.

Ned was sat on the path behind the last of the benches laughing. Tears running uncontrollably down his face. He wasn't sure when he had started to laugh but he knew what he was laughing at. Dancing on the bench above his head were two of the fattest bottoms he had ever seen, one male, one female. He had seen loads of bums before, of both genders, but these two creased him as they wobbled and flopped about.

"Look Jacko," he laughed, "look, it's a pair of jogging bottoms Hee! Hee! Hee! Look Jacko look."

Jacko did not look and, indeed, did not seem remotely interested. He was making his own fun leaping on and off the bench and flapping his arms. Crak! Crak! Crak! He called as he flapped up and down.

Vicar Howells was down on all fours sniffing the knees and inside leg of an attractive Scandinavian girl, who didn't seem to mind at all.

A baton waving, joyous Aldo urged his men on to a level of performance that they had never achieved before. In thirty years of conducting he had never heard one of his bands play so brilliantly. His audience were having a wonderful time. They were leaping around, laughing, dancing in the rain, and to his music. The fact that most of them were naked did not matter one bit and they were all ignoring the instructions from the helicopter above them to "PLEASE LEAVE BY THE MAIN GATE – PLEASE DON'T PANIC – PLEASE LEAVE QUIETLY."

The words were wasted. The mob creating happy mayhem at the bandstand, would be – later. For the time being they were never likely to panic, be quiet or have any intention of leaving – by any gate. It was party time!

19

The party at the bandstand was reaching unprecedented climaxes. With so much nakedness and liberated spirits abound it was little wonder that many couples took the opportunity to get it together. Never did the phrase multiple orgasm have so much meaning. The Danish police, realising that the euphoric erotica was confined to the area of the bandstand, concentrated their efforts on chasing and catching Ericsson. In a delirious and futile effort to make his escape he ran into the Balkan restaurant, and into Ferranti and Ames. All three were arrested. Frankie on suspicion of being involved with the chaotic drug dealing at the bandstand. Vaughan Ames on suspicion of being in the company of someone arrested on suspicion. The officer in charge also suspected that the blue and white bag Ames was carrying must be the one that held the cash that would pay for the drugs that were, once in Ericsson's bag. A mite circumstantial on the surface maybe, but a reasonably fair cop when you are desperate for a result. All three were carted off to the Hambrosgade police station loudly protesting their innocence, one in Swedish, one in Italian and the third in English.

At the station the police turned out Ames's bag and discovered that it contained nothing more than some overnight clothes and a camera. A posse of police rushed back to Tivoli to search for the missing bag. Two young and eager policemen spotted it straightaway. It was on the floor underneath the last bench at the bandstand. The mayhem, still fuelled on high octane, best Colombian, and aided by Adlo's band playing out of their skins, showed no sign of abating but the torrential downpour had. With outstanding will power and amazing devotion to their duties, the young men chose to ignore the pornographic performances taking place under their very noses. They decided to check the contents of the bag right there, so as not to look fools for the second time back at the police station. They emptied the bag's contents on to the ground. All they found were, toiletries, a black shirt, a pair of black socks, a clerics white dog collar and, two hard porn magazines. Their disappointment was edible. There was no drug money and they'd already bought the magazines.

Ned was still sat on the floor and witnessed the search but, for the moment, it failed to attract his attention. Just above him was a much more interesting scene. The two, fat, flabby, naked arses continued to wobble about to the music. Ned was amusing himself by poking them in turn with a stick. Each poke brought a squeak. First a low, male squeak then a higher, female squeak. Tears of hysterical joy were streaming down his own cheeks. He decided to make this game more interesting by trying to jam the stick into the crevice of one of these wobbling, musical arses. Would the first stick to crevice docking produce a high squeak or a low squeak? He took aim but stopped in mid-stab. This was a great game. He turned to the two policemen grovelling on the floor next to him.

"Fancy a poke pal? Look! Like this." Ned stabbed at a wobbling crevice. The arse let out a high squeak and the stick held fast. "Bull's-eye," Ned shouted triumphantly. "Hey! that's the vicar's bag. Bugger off and find something else to play with."

The vicar was oblivious to the fact that his bag had undergone a police inspection. He had been dragged from the inside leg of the girl he was sniffing by a young Dane. The Dane might have been studying carnal knowledge, and had decided that she would make a great text book. Howells opted for enjoying the concert.

Aldo's men were now into the tune that Miller wrote to remind him of a hotel telephone number, back home in Pennsylvania.

Howells, dancing on a bench along with the rest of the fans, soon realised that when a bell rang they all had to shout the number out. Here it came again.

Dah Deedum Dah Deedum Daah – Dah
Dah Deedum Dah Deedum Daah – Dah
Dah Deedum Dah Deedum Daah – RING PENNSYLVANIA 65 O O O YEAH!

Howells continued to O O O with the rest of the mad, but merry crowd. Prosser continued to leap on and off his bench, flapping his arms and "CRAK"-ing. Ned continued to poke and prod the arses and the police continued their search for a blue and white bag that must still be somewhere in Tivoli.

They turned the place inside out. Emptying rubbish bins, crawling through hedges searching every restaurant, toilet, cabaret room, the lake and, at the exit, anyone who was leaving. There was no sign of the bag that they believed was holding the payment for the drugs.

Back at the police station on Hambrosgade the officer in charge of what, he thought, was going to be a major drugs bust, a feather in his cap, a fast track to promotion, held his head in his hands. It had all gone wrong. Frankie Ferranti had been released. Ericsson was gibbering like a lunatic and would probably not be charged with anything on grounds of insanity. All he had to do now was tell the man sat in front of him, the Englishman Ames, that he too could go. He was on the verge of telling Vaughan Ames that he could go when a young policeman entered the interview room. He walked over to the officer, whispered something to him and laid an envelope down on the desk. The officer instantly perked up.

He now looked at Ames with eyes much brighter than they were a few moments ago. Opening the envelope he removed the photographs that were inside.

"Well! Well! Mr. Ames. It seems that one of my junior officers had the foresight and good police sense to develop the film that was in your camera."

The officer in charge looked again at the half a dozen colour photographs that he now spread out before him. "Hmmm, interesting," he smiled. Not a benevolent smile but an 'I've got you, you bastard', smile.

Ame's recognised the photographs that he had taken at the hotel earlier that evening. His mouth opened as though to offer his defence but no words of explanation would come out. His jaw had dropped too low to assist his tongue.

"Observe, Mr. Ames". The officer held up the photograph of Ned. "You have obviously taken this photograph whilst lying on the floor. But what a poor photographer you are. You have not angled the camera enough to get the mans head and shoulders in. The subject is clearly a man for, as you and I can both see, he has an erection. A fine erection if I may say so. One that I would be proud of myself in fact. Perhaps it was the sight of this fine erection that caused you to forget to get the man's face in the picture? No matter."

Ames's tried once more to explain, but now his voice box would not work.

"And this one Mr. Ames." Now it was a picture of the grotesque Sadie Wienburger. "Again you appear to be on the floor when taking this photograph. But this is a far more interesting snap shot. This time a female, lying on her back. And we can tell that this is a female can't we Mr. Ames? Not only are her legs in the air but, also, her night-dress has been lifted and pushed up by – A DOG Mr. Ames. A dog which has burrowed deep inside the lady's night-dress and can be now seen – well? how else can I put it? – licking her extremely ample breasts."

If Vaughan Ames's jaw needed to drop any lower it would have to be dislocated. His blood was running colder than the North Sea in a January gale. He was in a state of deep, deep shock.

"You see Mr. Ames we are very liberal minded here in Copenhagen. We understand that this sort of thing goes on. Goes on Mr. Ames, but behind closed doors or in private clubs. Not, Mr. Ames, in the corridor of, what looks like, a respectable and reputable Copenhagen hotel. No doubt the owners of the hotel will have something to say on the subject of pressing their own charges when we locate them. In the meantime I shall hold you here overnight for further questioning. I can see that you are in no state to continue at this moment. But I believe, Mr. Ames, that the top of your silver grey hair is just the tip of a large pornographic iceberg. One which I shall, in time, get to the bottom of."

Ames did not hear the last of the officers words. He had collapsed across the interview desk.

20

At Maxine's Bar on Colbjornsensgade the nine o'clock floor show was nearing its climax. A tall dark skinned girl with jet-black hair swept and tied tightly back off her face had removed all except a sequinned thong. She was now playing with a long phallic handle attached to, what looked like, a gambling machine. The machine was festooned with pulsating lights. The more erotically the girl played with its handle the faster its lights pulsated. She writhed and wriggled over and around it, licking her fingers and 'ooo-ing' as she caressed the large red ball on its top. Finally she stood astride this handle and grabbing the red ball with both hands she 'oooed' her way up it until her feet were off the ground. Her weight forced the handle slowly downwards until it was parallel with the floor. The sides of the machine then collapsed to reveal the glistening body of a naked man. Blue eyes, blond hair, obviously strong but without the bulging muscular appearance that turn women more off than on.

The man, without saying one word, instantly made his audience aware that whilst HE was completely naked SHE was not. Was this fair? he mimed. Should this injustice be allowed? His audience were now beginning to sit up and take notice, much more notice than previously.

In the friendly and free spirited city of Copenhagen a night-club floor show needed to be imaginative and tantalising in order to capture the jaded imaginations of its businessmen clientele. The blond hunk ran his hands over the girls upper body in a mock seeking of evidence of clothing. There was, of course, nothing to be found on her back. The evidence of his hands and, wide eyes also revealed absolutely nothing on her front – especially her breasts.

But wait! What's this?

Every pair of eyes followed his, and he ran his fingers down her body to the sequinned thong, the last line of defence that protected her from –.

Hearts began beating with eager anticipation. More than one pacemaker was close to overload as blond hunk knelt down and with teeth and index fingers, slowly removed this last vestige of clothing from her beautiful body. There followed an act which can only be described as – in fact cannot be described, not here on these pages. You will, dear reader, have to wait for that more salacious and adult piece of work from your author which is destined to reach the shelves of underground book shops at a later date. In the meantime it is sufficient to say that nothing was left to test even the most jaded of businessman's imaginations.

Throughout the show no-one in the audience looked at the girls eyes. Had anyone in the club that evening bothered to avert their own eyes from those parts of her body that they were riveted on, they would have noticed that the girl's attention was not wholly on the job in hand. Her gaze was frequently drawn towards the door that led punters into the cabaret room.

The note she had left at the Plaza had clearly stated 8.30. He was almost an hour late. Perhaps they had got to him already and he was now just one more victim. This show was almost at an end. She would then have, barely, twenty minutes before a repeat performance. If he was not here by then she would assume the worst. In the clubs foyer she heard laughter. The door to the cabaret room swung open. Ned, Prosser and the vicar each made an enthusiastic entrance – just as blond hunk was making his.

"Jees vicar, they love your bag don't they?" Ned laughed. "That's the second time you've had to turf it out tonight."

"Love me, love my bag. Bless you my son. Bless you my son. Bless you my son." Vicar Howells followed Ned into the club offering Papal Blessings to all. "Bless you my son, and especially to you my sweet young thing."

Jack Prosser followed behind with a grin on his craggy face that looked as though it had been chiselled on and could be permanent. The vicar and Prosser were stopped in their tracks when they bumped into Ned who had spotted the floor show.

"Dogs bollocks! Look at those two, they're having a –"

"Shall I find you a table sir. Somewhere where you can enjoy our entertainment more comfortably."

The trio, still fired up and happy on Hans Krog's corporate conviviality, were led away from the bright lights of the cabaret floor to a dimly lit, table in the corner of the room.

"Table for three will do pal. There's six seats here"

"You and your friends have no escorts?"

"No! Just me and the lads, my lovely boy."

"The Gold Card you left with us at reception ensures that, here at Maxine's, you will receive only the very best of what we can offer. I shall arrange for three beautiful young ladies to join you and you will of course only be drinking the very best champagne."

"Woar! Champagne. Absolutely my lovely boy, but let's have three pints of your very best lager as openers eh!"

"We only serve lager in jugs sir."

"Right! Give us three jugs then pal."

"They ARE litre jugs – of premium lager sir."

"Oh! Right! Better bring us two each then. And don't forget the champers. Bring on the champers and the tidy tarts, eh! vic?"

"Woar! indeed Mr. Dobson. Let us drink champagne from glass slippers. Bless your slippers my son. Bless your slippers and your tidy tarts. Woar! indeed, indeed."

Jack Prosser just grinned.

The floor show ended in an explosion of smoke bombs, lights and the throb of an anonymous piece of disco music to which blond hunk pumped in perfect tempo. The couple were dragged from the floor, still in situ copula, by a brace of monstrously over-bodied, ebony skinned, males wearing very little over their genitalia for the all too obvious reason that their genitalia appeared to be very little. The ebonies were a double helping of 260 pounds of dynamite with hardly a fuse between them.

With the floor show over for the time being the area was now available for discoing couples to leap up and thrust their parts at each other. The floor soon became an amalgam of assorted gyrating shapes and invented techniques fused together by that most super of all super-glue – lust. Two stunningly attractive girls emerged from the shadows and, with no murmur of complaint from either man, whisked the vicar and Prosser away from their table to the dance floor.

"Hey! You bastards! Where's mine?" Ned was about to get up to follow them when his lap was filled by the firm, and young bottom of the dark skinned girl who had so delightfully entertained the audience a few moments earlier. She was now wearing a red, satin basque with matching high heeled shoes. Wrapping her arms around him, she looked deep into his eyes.

"Hello. I'm Margaretha." She pressed her mouth gently onto his. The kiss, with just a hint of tongue, dispelled his annoyance and sent his imagination off on a journey of promiscuous possibilities. Their mouths parted, the girl pressed her cheek onto his and whispered. "You must be careful, be very careful."

"Oh! Righto. I'll get a packet of three from the bog, before we leave."

"No You do not understand. You do not need condoms."

"OH! RIGHTO RIGHTO MY LOVELY GIRL."

"NO! NO! Listen," she breathed, "they have already killed my boyfriend. You may be next."

"WHA –?"

This time Margaretha crashed her mouth onto his. This time, with Ned's mouth still wide open in stifled exclamation she sank her tongue deep inside, thus preventing any further vocal outbursts. At the same time she wriggled and pressed her buttocks around the apex of Ned's thighs until the ever-hardening lump inside his trousers confirmed that his libido was back to ruling his head. She slowly eased her mouth back but held her lips close to his, ready to attack his tonsils at a moment's notice.

"There is a man, a powerful and evil man. His power and wealth comes from controlling the gambling, prostitution and drug dealing that goes on in the major cities of Europe, including the U.K. He is a very secretive man. Not even the police know his true identity. Only his most trusted people are allowed to see him. Most of his employees know him only as The Voice." She paused for any sign of recognition on Ned's face. There was none. The girl continued. "This man puts no value on other people's lives. Anyone outside his inner circle who, like my Jurgen, discovers his identity is killed. He is an Englishman. His name is –."

Ned quickly placed his forefinger over Margaretha's lips. To a newspaperman facts and knowledge are the very lifeblood of a good scoop. In this instance Ned realised that the up-coming fact about to emerge from her may well result in his own lifeblood being spilt, to the point of his termination.

"Hold up. What's any of this got to do with me?"

"This afternoon you were being watched by one of Hans Krog's men."

"Hans Krog?"

"He owns Euro-Scan, a cable television company. Krog and The Voice are business associates."

"So?"

"Jurgen, my boyfriend, also discovered that Krog had done a deal with some people in your country."

"A deal?"

"Krog has friends in most of the Governments of Europe as well as your own Houses of Parliament. A group of, what your papers call Euro-sceptics were promised that the second Danish referendum on the

Treaty of Maastricht would return a –"

"A YES VOTE. YES! YES! YES! I WAS right after all" Ned's joy and jubilation were heading towards unconfinement until Margaretha, again, plunged her mouth onto his before grabbing his ears and hissing.

"No! NO! NO! They paid millions of pounds to Krog to get a 'NO' vote. They wanted the Treaty to be disrupted, held up, even abandoned altogether but Krog cheated on them."

Margaretha sensed that Ned was about to speak again. She cupped his face in her hands and with a most pleading look from her deep brown eyes that could not have possibly been acted said.

"Please! Please keep your voice down. We are both in danger here but you have a way out. You will soon be on a plane and out of this country. Tonight we must not draw attention to ourselves. Act naturally. Kiss me again."

This time Ned was ready for it and, for a full minute gave as good as he got. But this time, for the second time in his, snogging, groping, brazenly bonking anything in a skirt, life, he felt a glow – a warmth. Something like the feeling he got when Rosie gazed at him from behind the bar at the tip. Could Edward Dobson be falling in love again? Their mouths parted again. Ned was the first to speak.

"So, what about the football team?"

"What football team?"

"Denmark winning the European cup. Didn't they get that as a prize for the YES vote on Maastricht?"

"I do not know what you are talking about. None of this has anything to do with football. It was just business as far as Krog was concerned. You have a saying in your country – A gentleman's word is his honour – is that right?"

"Yeee-es," Ned said reluctantly. "I suppose it depends on the gentleman the word comes from."

"My Jurgen went with the rest of The Voice's European team to a hospitality weekend at Krog's headquarters in Gothenburg. The Voice was there but none of the team was allowed to see him. He spoke to them from another part of the building through a sound system. Jurgen was not well before he went. He had an upset tummy. During the party he suddenly became desperate for a – how do you say in English? –"

"A dump?" Ned offered.

"I think so. In his hurry he went into the Executive toilets by mistake. Just as he got into the cubicle Krog and The Voice came in. He heard Hans Krog boasting to The Voice that he had broke his word on a deal he had done with an honourable English gentleman and how he had sent the man a letter thanking him for his money – the letter was written in Swedish Krog thought that was a very funny thing to do. Krog addressed The Voice by his real name. My Jurgen was very frightened."

"I'll bet he was. The poor bugger must have crapped himself."

"I think that he did."

"Was that how they found out that he was there?"

"No, he held on until they had left but there are cameras everywhere at Krog's headquarters."

"Oh! Tough luck. So who is this 'Honourable English gentleman'? There can't be many of them left."

"He works at the British Foreign Office. His father is one of the main leaders of the group. His father is a wealthy landowner and handed over two million pounds of his money as part of his share in this deal. Krog hates the English. He just could not stop repeating the story of how he had dishonoured an honourable Englishman. My Jurgen told me his name. It was a strange name I could not understand it so I asked him to write it down. I have it here."

She slipped her hand into the top of her basque and retrieved a slip of paper which she handed to Ned. The name on the paper, WILLIAM FORS-BOWERS, hammered into Ned's bloodshot eyes. This time Margaretha could not fail to notice a sign of recognition that had been missing earlier.

"You know this man?"

"Know him?" Ned squeaked. He wanted to shout but a squeak was all he was allowed under the dangerous circumstances that Margaretha had laid on him. "Know him?" Ned repeated. "He's Randolph's son. Randolph, the bastard, has thrown away my inheritance. Two million quid that should have come to me not gone to some sleazball foreigner. That money was mine, I've earned it. I was the one who put up with his crazy daughter and his granddaughter, my wife by the way, for endless, mind numbing, years. I'll kill the little shit. I'll strangle him with his own, tweedy, plus fours. The Bastard The Bastard The Bastar –"

His mouth filled with her soft probing tongue. She sucked at his lips, forced her mouth into his, picked up his left hand and cupped it over her right breast. Ned could feel her nipple hardening. All thoughts of sending Randolph Fors-Bowers to burn in the fires of Hell were vanquished. Edward Dobson was, for the moment, in heaven.

Ned had no cause to worry over the state of Randolph's finances. Two million pounds was small change. Randolph Fors-Bowers was worth more than Ned could dream of in the wildest of his wild dreams.

On the dance floor of Maxine's Mr. Jack "Birdman" Prosser was establishing himself in a world that, until that evening, had been a strange and alien place. A place that, for him was best left alone.

That evening though, and with the assistance of an amazing burst of energy and a complete lack of his usual self consciousness, he was strutting his funky stuff like a good 'un. I fear that strutting may be putting too fine a point on Jack's interpretation of a disco movement. Perhaps clumping may be the adjective that we should be looking for. In any event the Birdman and his permanent grin were having a great time. The Reverend Howells felt quite at home in the company of this pot of scantily clad, writhing female flesh. He swayed with effortless rhythmical ease around his escort. None of those jerky and wooden moves for him. He was Mr. Cool. Mr Clerically Cool. While others flayed their arms, attempted half hearted splits and generally ducked and dived, whenever it took their fancy, Rhys Howells remained – well, cool can be the only interpretation that covers it.

At one point he sashayed towards his adopted escort whilst at the same time slipping his hand inside his jacket pocket. He could have been a Casablancan Humphrey Bogart about to give out a 'here's looking at you kid'. Such was his cool and laid back style. His hand, his right hand, inside his right-hand pocket lighted upon a powder-like substance. When Ericsson's bullet had set free Krog's cocaine from the bag slung over Howells's shoulder, a few potent ounces of it had found its way into Howells's pocket. He took out a handful. Adopting the pose of a Spanish flamenco dancer he proceeded to sprinkle the powder into the ever narrowing space between him and his partner.

Ned's libido was dancing to a different rhythm. Love was in the air. The softness of Margaretha's lips, on his neck and cheeks, plus the bulge in his trousers, combined to press the point home. They had already finished one bottle of champagne. But as there were two more already chilling in ice buckets that didn't matter. Who was counting? Denzil's gold card could handle it – them – and much, much more.

Margaretha, being accustomed to sipping over priced house champagne with the club's customers, always made sure that the man on who's lap she was nestling got more than his share. With this customer she need not have bothered. Ned, in love or not, was known for taking a share that was at least equal to the sum of the shares of those drinking with him. On a one to one basis such as this it was split 70/30 in his favour.

In between sipping champagne and tonguing his tonsils, Margaretha had extracted a promise from him that, when he returned to the U.K. he would use all his powers, influence and contacts with the Gloucester police, to turn over Krog and The Voice and bring Jurgens' murderer to justice.

"Leave it to me sweetheart. I won't let you down. Trust me I'm a journalist." Gallant words, cynically spoken. Ned's powers, influence and contacts within any of H.M.'s police forces were nil. The courage he needed to turn in drug dealers and murderers was even less. When he returned to Copenhagen, as he knew he would one day, he would blag out some sort of story which would get him off the hook. Ned was never short of a story, real or imagined.

As Margaretha caressed his forehead and smothered his face in soft kisses she could see the floor manager signalling for her to prepare for the next show.

"I must go. I am on in a few minutes."

Suddenly, Ned felt a pang of jealousy. In the short time that she had been sat on his lap she had, as far as he was concerned, become HIS girl. Now HIS girl was about to rush off and bare everything to a roomful of ogling slimeballs. He did not feel too happy about it. He hung on to her waist with both arms in an effort to delay the inevitable.

"I must go. I must go."

But there was no rush, at least not as far as the punters were concerned. They were being treated to an extra cabaret performance. One not advertised in the original programme of events.

The Reverend Rhys Howells had decided that when it came to stripping in public he was every bit as good as the next woman. He was down to his final garment, a pair of black satin boxer shorts covered in bright red hearts and lips. Rhys Howells, vicar of St Tyllow's, Church Street, Little Hardwicke, England, was about to become the star turn at Maxine's Bar, Colbjornsengade, Copenhagen, Denmark, and may even get a seasons booking for his efforts.

21

As hangovers go the ones that Ned, Prosser and the vicar were about to wake up to would be nothing short of monstrous. Sorry, did I include Mr. Edward Dobson in that union of thumping heads? That, 'I'll never touch another drop as long as I live' group. How, stupendously stupid of me to forget the fact that our hero Ned has the constitution of an alien. Of one who is not of this terrestrial globe. Of one who's body and all the vital organs contained therein are impervious to attack from anything, legal or illegal. A body that just does not react in the way that is expected and accepted by those of us who are mere mortals on this planet that we call Earth.

Ned woke as he always does regardless of the previous evening's excesses, as bright as a button at precisely 7.15 a.m. The fact that Central European Time was not synchronized with British Summer Time made no difference. The world's travellers may suffer from jet lag, time zone disorientation, sudden and gastronomically upsetting changes of diet but not Ned. Definitely not Ned. On this Friday morning he woke with a clear head and as sharp as a tack. The overnight storm had cleared the air. He was hungry.

From somewhere on the floor, near the foot of his bed, he could hear snoring. He swung his legs over the bed and stood up. He saw the prostrate and near lifeless body of the vicar. He was wearing a pair of black satin shorts with bright red hearts and lips printed on them, nothing else. Beside him was his blue and white bag. It contained, as the Danish police and the doorman at Maxine's discovered the night before, his toiletries, a change of clothes and two adult magazines. His new light grey suit and the rest of his clothes were tied up in a bundle next to it. This bundle of clothes were the ones that he would have changed out of in the privacy of his hotel room, had he not already removed them at Maxine's Bar. Ned did not have to rack his brains to remember the finale of the night's entertainment. The three of them had been politely asked to leave the bar just after the vicar was seen jumping across the tables of the club completely naked waving his black satin shorts in the air and singing 'Onwards Christian soldiers'.

"Not a bad night eh! vic?" Ned nudged the vicars calf with his foot. There was no response. "Don't s'pose you fancy some grub then?"

The vicar did not. He didn't say as much but Ned just knew that the vicar would not be joining him for breakfast. "Well! Maybe the Birdman's up for it."

Ned showered, dressed and headed off towards Jack Prossers' room. But, banging on, kicking at, and shouting through the door of room 384 brought no reply, so he gave it up and went down to breakfast on his own.

In the breakfast room of the Plaza hotel Ned went for the closest he could get to a full greasy spoon start of the day. What he got was all too familiar to him. A fried breakfast, for sure, but sanitised and virtually greaseless. An identical twin to that which Gwendolyn serves up, every morning. Gwendolyn!! Oh God!, and Magenta, Randolph and the Record. Oh double triple quadruple God!!!! In an hour or so he'll be heading back to Gloucestershire and the same grinding, familiar routine.

And what of Randolph? Why did he send the vicar out so suddenly? Oh! Quintuple, sextuple, septuple GOD! If the old bugger has lost all his money in this stupid Euro scam and now expects to come and live with him at Monks End then the bastard has got another think coming. He's got no chance, and if he thinks that he has then I'm off. Quicker than that bird at the strip joint got hers off last night. That bird? Margaretha, she was lovely. Deep brown eyes long legs smooth skin – ooh! Ned was suddenly covered in the warm and glowing passion he had felt for her. She was special. If this Randolph thing was going to end up pear shaped then he would be back in Copenhagen before the weekend, probably for good. Wait up? What about Rosie, she was special too. Maybe he could alternate, intermingle a bit. Six months with Rosie and six months with Margaretha. Earning a few bob as a foreign correspondent on either side of the North sea. The idea had a lot going for it. He stabbed a sausage with his fork dipped it into the yolk of his egg, sucked at it slowly, before biting the end off.

In room 386 of the Plaza Hotel, Jack Prosser was sat on the edge of his bed in his matching brown socks and pants. He was bent forward leaning on his large, boney knees staring at the deep red carpet that covered the floor of his hotel room. The colour of the carpet mirrored the mist that was swirling around in front of his eyes. He had a hangover. There was absolutely no doubt about that. You can't have a mate like Ned to drink with and not get to appreciate the significance of a bloody good hangover. The worse you felt the next morning the better the time you must have had the night before.

This morning it was different. This hangover was not like any other. It had an added ingredient. A thumping head, of course. Churning guts, only to be expected. But the depression? This extra sensation had never been a factor in the first stages of the morning after the night before. This was an unwelcome first for Birdman Jack Prosser. The phrase 'cold turkey' only had one meaning to him. Boxing Day dinner, the day after Christmas Day. On that day, at No. 5 the Cottages Monks End and every other house in the village, the family meal would be; cold turkey, home made, giant sized, chips and an assortment of pickles. To Jack the phrase cold turkey simply meant great big slices off the breast of an already cooked bird.

In his room at the Plaza Hotel one thought was making a most urgent effort to force its way through the red mist. Where did he leave the bag that he had to take back to Gloucester. The one that Sophie had made him promise to bring back to her.

He should never have mixed his drinks. Champagne and lager. Champagne? What was he doing drinking that stuff? Where was he drinking that stuff? Wherever it was had music, flashing lights, explosions and naked girls. Was that at the bandstand, or at that other place? What other place? Some club somewhere. The bandstand, that's where he had the bag last. But there was music, flashing lights, explosions and naked girls there too. All these thoughts were jumbling together in his confused brain. Someone had replaced his memory with a plate of scrambled eggs. Where could the bag be? He repeated the question to himself, as he ambled towards the door. He couldn't remember a knock but he was going to open it anyway.

"Jees Jacko, you look like dried dog shit." Jack stared vacantly at Ned as he pushed past him into the room. "You'd better shut the door pal. If you stay there in those baggy Y fronts and socks you could get arrested, or propositioned. Strange mob in this town."

Jack closed the door then sagged into the armchair next to his bed. His was head full of confusion and his eyes full of red mist. Ned's head was clear and his eyes were sparkling. "So, you didn't fancy a greasy spoon breakfast then?" he continued.

"No."

"No? You must be starving, the energy you burned up last night."

"Eh?"

"Leaping on and off that bench in the Tivoli, waving your arms like a man possessed you were. And the disco – what a mover. Wait till I tell the lads at the Tip. They'll –"

"WHAT? – What was I doing at the Tivoli?" A hint of recollection began to appear through the red mist clouding Jack's eyes. "At the Tivoli – what did I do?"

The excesses of the previous night had done little to tarnish Ned's memory. "Well, you were jumping on and off a bench, flapping your arms like a dying chicken and shouting 'I'm a J – I'm a J'."

" 'I'm a J?' " Jack questioned.

"Yeah! Gord only knows why? What's J got to do with the price of cheese?"

The crack in the red mist widened just enough for Birdman Jack Prosser to see a vision. Now he knew where the bag was.

"I wasn't shouting J."

"No?"

"No! I was shouting JAY."

"That's what I said didn't I – J. Are you dull or what?"

"No! Not J – Jay, the bird Jay. J A Y." Jack felt obliged to spell the name out in order that there would be no more misunderstanding.

"Oh well, all right then you were flapping your arms about like a dying Jay. It's all the same to me pal. Anyway, you've missed breakfast but we can't miss the plane. We've got one hour to pack, check out and get to the airport." Ned started to leave Prosser's room.

"Airport?" Jack queried.

"Yes! Airport mate. Where the planes take off from. Randolph wants me back sharpish and the vicar's booked us out on the mid-day plane."

"Randolph who?" Jack's mist was still hovering.

"Randolph – Gwendo's old man you pillock. The rich git I've been trying to get back in with for the past million years. He's got something to tell me, and it had better not be what I think it is. Oh! and the vicar's collapsed at the foot of my bed. He could be unconscious for a month by the look of him. Out cold and flatter than a witch's tit. You'll have to help me get him dressed. We may have to carry the poor sod onto the aeroplane so put your skates on, we haven't got all day."

Before Ned had got back to his own room Jack Prosser was well on his skates. The blue and white bag that he had to take back to Sophie was still in the Tivoli

Gardens. The events of the evening were a bit hazy but he could now work it out. In the mayhem and confusion at the bandstand, someone had thrown a third bag down at his feet. THREE blue and white bags! That was one too many.

When a Jay bird comes across an abundance of food it takes what it wants then sets about hiding some for later. Fuelled up on lager and accidental cocaine Birdman Jack Prosser had picked one up, stood on the bench and tossed it into the branches of a nearby tree. There it would be safe from other hungry birds. Flapping his arms and imitating the "Crack! Crack!" of the Jay, he had leapt on and off his perch, the bench, calling out just as Ned had said; 'I'm a Jay – Crack! Crack! – I'm a Jay'.

The Danish police had searched thoroughly at ground level but not one pair of eyes had bothered to look up. People, even policemen, rarely look up.

Jack Prosser slipped into Tivoli, stood up on the bench and retrieved the bag. A few minutes later he was packing it into his suitcase in his room at the Plaza.

Ned was also trying to pack – the Reverend Rhys Howells into his trousers. As Ned knelt down in front of him the vicar was barely conscious and had no control over his limbs, or his stomach. The latter being determined to rid itself of all it contained, which it did so at regular intervals.

"Where the bloody hell is Prosser?" Ned cursed as another burst of bile like fluid pumped from the vicars sagging mouth. A knock on the door announced Prosser's arrival. Ned got up to let the Birdman in. He left the vicar with one leg inside his trousers, while the other one flapped aimlessly about, wondering why it had been left out in the cold.

"You're having a bit of trouble then?" Jack said, as he walked in.

"WE mate. WE are having a bit of trouble and, we will probably be having a bit of trouble for the best part of the day by the looks of him. Where have you been?

Help me get him half respectable or we are going to miss the plane."

"You've got puke down the front of your shirt."

"Don't worry pal, before we're finished you'll have your share."

Twenty minutes and a pint of reeking vomit later and Howells was propped up against the wardrobe, more or less ready to be removed from the building and take his chances with the outside world.

"Gord! You stink Jacko."

"So do YOU," Jack countered.

"Never mind. It might not notice under our jackets. Come on. You take one arm and I'll take the other. Once we get him on the plane he can sleep it off. Let's go."

With their luggage bags in one hand and the vicar in the other, the trio made reasonable progress along the corridor, until they approached room 384.

"Hark at the racket in there" Ned had hardly got the words out before the door to 384 was flung open. Two men came out. Elmer Weinburger was handcuffed between them. They were followed by two more, flanking Sadie. A third was dragging Mimi the poodle along at the end of a dog lead. Most of the racket was coming from Elmer.

"Son of a bitch Sadie! You said you'd given all that up."

"But it's not me I tell ya. It's not me." Sadie protested.

"Sure it's you, you wrinkled old whore. I'd recognise that arse anywhere – so would the whole of Goddam Texas."

The arresting officers and protesting defendants made their way down the corridor. Mimi the poodle made her own canine protest by crapping and peeing on the carpet at every opportunity.

"Jees! There are some strange people in this town Jacko, I'm coming back for a proper holiday one day."

Mimi the poodle was being dragged down the middle

of the corridor. With Ned and Jack Prosser holding him up on either side the semiconscious vicar was obliged to walk a similar path. His shoes squelching first in poodle shit and then in poodle piss. The upcoming aroma combined delightfully with that emitting from the trios puke covered shirts.

22

The concourse of Copenhagen airport was bustling with travellers. Hundreds of passengers were milling around. Some going to eat, some to buy duty free, some to reclaim the value added tax on goods bought in the city shops. Others were sat in rows of seats patiently waiting for their boarding call. Frankie Ferranti wasn't milling, or eating, or buying, or reclaiming. Neither was he patiently waiting. Frankie was stood. Stood in a telephone booth. Not talking, but listening as usual.

"Frankie! Frankie! My Italian marble mosaic. What went wrong? I could not believe my ears when I heard the news. But these were Frankie's plans, I said. His plans always go to plan. Frankie Ferranti has never yet let me down, I said. But Frankie, my sweet treaded grape, is there not a first time for everything? Are we, all of us, not allowed one mistake in our busy and stressful lives? My confidence in your ability remains unquestioned. You must not worry, dear boy. Worry brings on even more stress and that can be so self destructive, can it not my passionate slice of Parma Ham?"

Frankie's stress level rose. He began to worry, which increased his stress, as The Voice had predicted. Self-destruction may be just around the corner. Perhaps that's what The Voice expected of him. A vote of confidence from The Voice generally spelt trouble. He hoped that on this occasion it would not. The Voice continued; "You must take a rest dear boy. Do not return to England. You are booked on the next plane to Rome. You will find a first class ticket waiting for you at the Lufthansa booking desk. Enjoy the Italian sunshine. You are beginning to look as pale as porcelain. I prefer my men to be fit and bronzed – all over, dear boy – all over. If you come back to me fit and bronzed all over, you will make me very happy."

So there will be a price to pay, thought Frankie. Get fit, get bronzed, come back and get rogered. Ah well! It could have been worse.

"And Frankie." The Voices voice hardened. "While you are away recuperating you may rest assured that we shall recoup our money. Our one hundred thousand pounds is still missing. We SHALL retrieve it. Our man within the Danish police force is, even as I speak to you, making a copy of the police film of last nights debacle. We shall discover where our money went dear Frankie. Someone has it in their possession. They shall be hounded. Whoever dared to perpetrate such a criminal act shall pay dearly. Trust me Frankie. Trust me. Ciau!"

Frankie trusted him. No one steals from The Voice and gets away with it.

As he replaced the receiver he smelt a most obnoxious smell wafting into the booth. He turned and saw people with handkerchiefs held to their faces, apparently hurrying away from the source of the stink. Frankie took out his own handkerchief and followed them. Lucky for him the Lufthansa desk was in that direction. He not only left the smell behind but also the bag in Prosser's suitcase that was holding The Voice's money. He would never know how close he was to redeeming his reputation with his master and thus avoiding their next, anally painful, meeting.

"Nice of those people to let us have these seats," Jack said.

"Well, they could see that the vicar was a bit under the weather couldn't they. These Europeans could teach our lot a thing or two when it comes to good manners. I'll give them that."

As Ned, the vicar and Jack Prosser sat in the front row of the waiting area they failed to notice that rows of seats behind them had also become vacant. Large numbers of waiting passengers had suddenly decided to stretch their legs rather than sit near the three British travellers. The airport's Duty Sanitary Officer had been contacted and ordered to seek out the source of the stink. His orders were, to nullify the problem and return the atmosphere to its original aromatic fragrance. He sent out a team of cleaners with their trolleys loaded with sprays, assorted fragrances, disinfectants, mops and brushes. It did not take one of them long to discover the cause of the nasal discomfiture. A vicar, or priest, was sitting apparently asleep with his legs outstretched. The soles of his shoes were clearly visible. On them were large areas of brown stuff. The cleaner had seen enough of such brown stuff to immediately recognise it as dog shit. He was surprised that the two gentlemen sat next to the priest had not complained. The cleaner's job description did not include scraping, spraying and wiping the soles of the shoes of passengers, even if they were members of the clergy. He used his mobile phone to call his supervisor for guidance.

"Sir!" The Duty Sanitary Officer gently shook Rhys Howells on the shoulder to rouse him from his sleep. "Excuse me sir."

"It's no good mate," Ned offered, "he's knackered. He had a stormer last night. He's completely bollocksed, you won't get much out of him. What's your problem anyway?"

One of the DSO's problems was that he was trying to hold down his airport breakfast. There had been nothing wrong with the food. He, also, had had a stormer last night. He had been in the crowd at the bandstand that had got stoned. He had continued to party throughout the night. Somehow he managed to get to work on time and hoped that a breakfast would quell his nausea. He took out his handkerchief and held it up to his nose. It wasn't just the one smell coming from the crap on the bottoms of the vicar's shoes. There was a foul stink coming off all three of them. It clawed at the back of his throat. He felt as though he was going to throw up – he did.

His partly digested breakfast spewed out, hitting the vicar squarely on his bald head. The lumpy bits held fast, leaving the juices to trickle down the inside of the vicar's collar.

"Bloody hell mate," Ned protested, "you may not believe in the Almighty but you don't have to throw up all over one of his disciples."

"Whoooph." The man boffed a second time but there was little left inside his stomach. Most of its contents were now being worn by Howells, on his head. These last dregs fell more or less harmlessly onto the vicar's lap.

"Come with me." The DSO croaked. "You won't be allowed to board a plane in that condition. He," pointing at Howells, "will have to remove his shoes. He will have to walk in his socks."

Howells was just regaining consciousness as Ned and Jack Prosser lifted him up off his seat.

"OH MY GOODNESS!" His knees buckled. If it wasn't for Ned and Prosser holding on to him he would have collapsed in a pile. "My head, my head." Howells tried to put his hand up to his aching temple but Ned's arm was locked in his.

"I wouldn't put your hand up there for a bit if I were you vicar." Ned said, eyeing the regurgitated bits of food that were stubbornly staying put on Howells's forehead.

"Goodness! What's that terrible smell?"

"It's you mostly. Don't worry about it, we're going for a quick wash and brush up. Just keep moving as best you can."

* * *

"So, Mr Ames. We now have your accomplices in custody."

"My accomplices?" Ames protested. "MY accomplices? What are you talking about?"

"Not what Mr Ames, but who. And you know very well who we have arrested. You know them very well indeed."

181

"I told you. I haven't got the faintest idea what you are talking about," Ames said, arrogantly, "and I won't answer any of your questions until my solicitor arrives from England."

"Let us not play cat and mouse games Mr. Ames. Your camera contained a number of photographs of this lady." The officer pushed the photograph of Sadie across the desk. "Sadie Wienburger Mr. Ames. A convicted brothel keeper and star of more than a dozen pornographic films involving, as I'm sure you are aware, an assortment of animals. Mr. Wienburger, her husband, has confirmed that this is her. I will Mr. Ames, sooner or later, discover what your involvement was in this vile, pornographic ring," the officer said, stabbing his finger at the photo of Sadie's arse.

"It is all a mistake. A silly mistake."

"Ah! Mr. Ames. If I only had one Danish Kroner for each time that I heard that remark in this very room, I would be a rich man."

* * *

Ned, Jack and the vicar had been left sitting in a store room in the service area of Copenhagen's airport. Ned and Prosser had given up their shirts for cleaning. The vicar had only his black satin boxer shorts and black socks to cover his embarrassment. They had been assured by the Duty Sanitary Officer that their clothes would be returned to them washed and pressed in plenty of time for them to catch their plane to Heathrow.

For the second time that morning a tattoo on Rhys Howell's upper, left arm caught Ned's eye. It was a heart with a cupid's arrow through it. The name Gwendolyn curved underneath it. He had noticed it when he was trying to get the vicar dressed at the Plaza. But as the man was unconscious there was no way that he could inquire about it.

Now though, Howells was reasonably lucid and able to speak.

"Er! Nice girl was she Vic?" Ned, cautiously, offered the question whilst pointing at the tattoo.

"Oh!" Howells instinctively covered it up with his right hand but he knew that the game was well and truly up.

"I'm afraid I have something to tell you Mr. Dobson. A sort of, confession."

There followed a confession which, as it unfolded, caused both Ned's and Jack Prosser's eyes to grow to the size of saucers. They sat as though stunned whilst listening to Howells's story. When the vicar had finished it was Jack who was the first to break the tense and incredulous silence.

"So, you and Ned's mother-in-law had a –"

"An assignation. A love affair."

"But if Ned's wife, Magenta, is your daughter that makes you Ned's –"

Jack was about to say the words, Father-in-Law, when he received a look from Ned that could only have meant. "YOU DARE – YOU BLOODY DARE."

Birdman Jack Prosser bloody dared not – so he shut up.

On the plane that took them away from Copenhagen and back to Heathrow, Ned sat in the window seat morose and sulky. He refused his in flight meal and spoke not a word to anyone. He was already deep in one of his 'moments'. Black dog had arrived at 30,000 feet.

The Reverend Rhys Howells was feeling better. Confession, as he constantly reminded his parishioners, is good for the soul. His spirit was up. He had drunk two large glasses of red wine and was already fancying one of the stewardesses. Jack Prosser had insisted on the aisle seat and, to take his mind of his fear of flying, he talked and talked, just as he had done on the flight out. Not though, on the Treaty of Maastricht. Throughout the flight to Heathrow the vicar received ecumenical, chapter and verse on religious theory. Jack Prosser, ornithologist, expounded at length on whether the Catholic Church was indeed, the one, true apostolic

183

faith. It may one day occur to Jack that the more he was prepared to risk flying the more knowledgeable he became.

Apart from Ned's moody, Prosser's theory and Howells's lechery, the flight home was quite uneventful.

23

At the Heathrow baggage carousel Jack Prosser was standing with Rhys Howells waiting for the bags to emerge. The vicar's only luggage was the blue and white flight bag, which he was carrying over his shoulder. He had been assigned to collect Ned's case whilst Ned made three phone calls. Prosser edged nervously backwards and forwards. He was still in a state of tension from the flight out of Denmark. He still had to deliver that bag, that damned blue and white bag, to Sophie at the Record. His case appeared at the top of the carousel. He grabbed it. Close behind was Ned's.

"That's his." Jack indicated to Howells.

On the coach down the motorway to Gloucester Ned said not a word. His depression had been converted to anger and hatred. The first of his phone calls had been to the Fors-Bower's Estate. Three times he had dialled the number. Each time he had got the same result. Number unobtainable. His hatred for Randolph was becoming obsessive. The bastard must have had his phone cut off. He has lost all his cash on that Euroscam. He sent the vicar to bring me back home because he's destitute and wants to live in the spare room at Monks End.

BOLLOCKS! NO CHANCE! To make matters even worse the randy vicar sat next to him was the father of his wife. A wife who spent three evenings a week on the game.

Oh dear! Life can be so cruel.

Randolph Fors-Bowers was not broke or in need of somewhere to live. He was not about to become homeless and had no more thoughts of living with Ned, Gwendolyn and Magenta than flying to the moon. As soon as he knew the reporter was on his way

185

back to England and no longer a risk to his reputation as a respected landowner, Randolph had changed his telephone number. His secretary and estate managers were instructed not to accept calls from Dobson, Gwendolyn, Magenta or, even Rhys Howells. Randoph Fors-Bowers would not shed a tear if he never saw any of them again.

The second call had been to Denzil. To tell him that there was no big international news story. The Record will have to rely on Denzil's original plan of serialising the Treaty of Maastricht – in English and whatever else. Riveting stuff eh?

The third of Ned's calls had been to Charlie Harries, the landlord at the Tip. Ned had asked Charlie to pick them up at the coach stop in Gloucester. Ned was going straight to Charlie's pub to get pissed out of his brains. Then Rosie was going to get the bonking of a lifetime. Brewers droop had never dared to visit itself upon Edward Dobson. After that – well, maybe it would be time to move on.

The ever reliable Charlie was waiting for them as they got off the coach. Cases were stowed in the back of his Volvo and they climbed in. Ned sat in the front, Jack and the vicar in the back.

"All back to my place for a beer?" Charlie asked.

"ER! Not for me thank you," Howells said. "If you wouldn't mind dropping me off at the vicarage I would be very grateful. I have to prepare for morning service you know."

"Of course vicar, of course. So it's one for the vicarage and three of us to the pub then."

"No thanks Charlie," Jack Prosser interrupted. "I've got a bit of shopping to do in Woolies. I'll be down for a pint later."

Charlie Harries didn't even consider asking Ned if he was coming to the pub.

At the front door of the vicarage Mrs Mumford was waiting for her much admired and loved employer. A beaming smile on her round face and her arms folded just under her heaving breasts. HE WAS BACK.

"I've got a joint of lamb roasting in the oven, some of my home made apple crumble and there's a glass of your favourite port poured and ready for you on the mantelpiece."

"Thank you Mrs. Mumford. You are so very kind."

What a pity, Rhys Howells thought, what a pity I don't fancy her. If only she looked a little, just a little, like Tania.

Jack Prosser got out of Charlie's car and immediately went to the Record's offices. The door to reception was unlocked. He entered and rang the bell. No one answered. He checked his watch it was ten past five. The rest of the staff may have left but Sophie would often work over. He guessed that she was in another part of the building. He took the blue and white bag from out of his case and placed it on her desk. That was it, done, finished. His nightmare had ended. Never again would he let that young lady talk him into anything EVER.

Jack Prosser closed the door behind him and headed for home and his beloved wife Agnes. He was going to give her such a hug.

* * *

Ned dropped his case in the bar of the Tip and eyed Rosie with a look of determined passion.

"You're back early," she said. "We thought you were over there 'till the weekend. What are you having?"

"I'll have a large one," Ned said, staring at the front of her T-shirt. "The one on the left will do for starters."

"Two pints of best then," Rosie countered with a twinkle.

* * *

In his profuse and immaculate office Densil Wynstanly

sat at his desk, head bowed and sweating profusely. In his hand was a letter from his bank manager. The letter had been delivered by hand, as an indication of it's urgency. He had read it three times. It was not getting any better. Each reading made him more listless and dispirited. The letter was long winded and in parts almost apologetic. The bones of it were as clear as day. The company's overdraft had reached an unprecedented and unauthorised level. Mainly by some extravagant spending on his Gold credit card, in Copenhagen. The overdraft must be reduced by 50,000 pounds immediately. If this request could not be met by noon the following day then the Bank would have no other option than to foreclose.

Denzil rose wearily from his sweat stained desk. This letter and the phone call from Dobson were the last of two very heavy straws. His battle with The Clarion and Vaughan Ames no longer mattered. He closed his office door for what must be the last time. As he passed through reception he spotted a blue and white bag on Sophie's desk.

"Sophie," he called. "Sophie are you still here?"

Picking up the bag he walked around the offices calling her name. She was not in the studio, or the sales office, or the distribution office, or, even the ladies toilet. The building was deserted. Everyone had gone home. He put the bag down. It's contents may give some clue to it's owner. He unzipped the bag. He could not believe his eyes. Money, lots of money. Cash, notes, bundles and bundles of them. He sat down and counted. 50,000, 80,000, 100,000 pounds in used notes. No name or address or clue as to their owner. One hundred thousand pounds – orphaned!!!

He considered his options. Hand the cash to the police or hide it in a secret bank account. He considered the letter from the company's bank – no more consideration was necessary.

* * *

"We shall get our money back. Trust me Frankie, trust me."

* * *

END